THE PRECIPICE

The Texas Pan American Series

the
PRECIPICE
(EL BORDO)

by SERGIO GALINDO

translated by
JOHN *and* CAROLYN BRUSHWOOD

with an Introduction by
JOHN BRUSHWOOD

DRAWINGS BY LUIS EADES

UNIVERSITY OF TEXAS PRESS, AUSTIN AND LONDON

The Texas Pan American Series is published with the assistance of a revolving publication fund established by the Pan American Sulphur Company and other friends of Latin America in Texas. Publication of this book was also assisted by a grant from the Rockefeller Foundation through the Latin American translation program of the Association of American University Presses.

Standard Book Number 292–78408–2
Library of Congress Catalog Card Number 74–83762
Printed by The University of Texas Printing Division, Austin
Bound by Universal Bookbindery, Inc., San Antonio

For Angela

INTRODUCTION

Sergio Galindo creates a fiction-
al world using the Mexican background that is familiar to him,
but his readers are less aware of the setting than of the people
who stand out against it. The artist's emphasis is on re-creating
the complexity of human relationships, and particularly on
showing the individual's yearning for personal fulfillment. It
is this emphasis on people (rather than on places) that may
be used as an identifying characteristic of Galindo and several
other novelists of approximately the same age—Luisa Josefina
Hernández, Emilio Carballido, Sergio Fernández, Vicente
Leñero.

The three best-known Mexican novelists of our time are
Agustín Yáñez (1904), Juan Rulfo (1918), and Carlos Fuentes
(1929). Their birth dates give a fair indication of the age
spread among novelists who are writing at this time. Galindo,
who was born in 1926, belongs to the youngest group of writers
who are firmly established. There is, of course, an even younger group, just now beginning to define their literary characteristics.

Yáñez, Rulfo, and Fuentes are all novelists who, like Galindo,
know how to use typically Mexican material without being
simply picturesque. They move out from the particular to the
universal. But Galindo is different because his primary emphasis is on the people rather than the scene. The non-Mexican
reader of Yáñez or Rulfo or Fuentes is likely to remark that
they deal with a most extraordinary world—this in spite of
their skillfully developed and eminently human characters.
Galindo's non-Mexican reader, on the other hand, is more like-

ly to comment on how intensely human the people are, in spite of his unmistakably Mexican settings.

Mexican fiction, for three decades after the end of the Revolution in 1917, tended to be nationalistic, even chauvinistic. The authors dealt with the traumatic experience of the Revolution itself and with the social problems it brought into focus. Occasionally, one of them was able to transcend the limitations of this obsession and use the themes to make a work of art. Mariano Azuela did it, for example, in *Los de abajo (The Underdogs)* and two or three other novels. And there was a moment in the twenties when a few sophisticated young writers experimented with avant-garde fiction. But the need to comprehend the national experience was overwhelming, and aesthetic considerations were often forgotten or purposely ignored.

Yáñez's *Al filo del agua (The Edge of the Storm)*, published in 1947, was a literary breakthrough because the author knew, and still knows, how to be very Mexican and very universal at the same time. His places, people, and problems are all clearly Mexican, he even deals with the causes of the Revolution; yet readers of any time and place can identify with the basic human qualities that are apparent within the particular situation.

By the time Rulfo published *Pedro Páramo* in 1955, there was no longer any question about treating national themes with artistic sensitivity. Yáñez had already experimented with style and structure without being considered "arty". His interior monologues, dream sequences, and poetic prose vignettes serve to re-create Mexican reality more accurately than memoirs and tales of quaint people and places. Rulfo goes even farther. He brings to life the personalistic and domineering "boss" of a region, the *cacique*. In doing so he makes extensive use of time distortion, free association, and a variety of points of view to tell a story that moves beyond the ordinary line between life and death and asks what life really is.

There is a feeling of magic about *Pedro Páramo* because reality in the novel does not fit the pattern of reality as we normally think of it. Some of the same effect is found in Fuentes' *La región más transparente (Where The Air Is Clear)*, published in 1958, and in Elena Garro's *Los recuerdos del porvenir (Recollections of Things to Come)*, one of the prize-winning novels of 1963. In other words, one of the characteristics of the contemporary novel is that things happen that cannot be explained scientifically. Sometimes Galindo achieves a similar effect by telescoping time, or by projecting reality as seen by one person onto reality as seen by another person. But his irrealities never surprise, because they become a part of a total characterization and are not emphasized as unreal.

Fuentes is undoubtedly the most spectacular novelist of the moment. His books are heroic, broad canvases. His techniques are very experimental, and always interesting though not uniformly effective. His treatment of Mexico is a tumultuous love affair. He caresses her, quarrels with her, makes love to her, points out her shortcomings. His best-known novels scream their Mexicanism. *La región más transparente* rapidly became one of the most controversial novels ever published in Mexico. The discussion concerned the accuracy of the young author's interpretation of Mexico and the usefulness of his experimentation.

A much quieter event was the publication in the same year of Galindo's *Polvos de arroz (Rice Powder)*. Both Fuentes and Galindo had published collections of short stories that are really exercises preliminary to their actual literary careers. The contrast between their first major works not only defines Galindo as a novelist, but indicates the general character of the works of those writers already mentioned who join him in their tendency to be less flamboyant, more intimate.

Polvos de arroz is the story of a provincial spinster who has sacrificed her possible fulfillment for the sake of her family. Late in life she enters into a lonely-hearts correspondence with a young man in Mexico City. Hope flickers briefly, but only because her yearning blinds her to reality. Galindo wrote this short novel with amazing gentleness and simplicity that caused Emmanuel Carballo, a very exacting Mexican critic, to call it "one of the most beautiful written in twentieth-century Mexico." An approximation of this protagonist appears in several places in Galindo's work. It is a characterization that synthesizes the novelist's principal thematic material: the reconciliation of individual fulfillment with the exigencies of human relationships.

In consecutive years, Galindo published *La justicia de enero (Capricious Justice)* and *El Bordo (The Precipice)*. In both novels he handles more intricate relationships, sharpens his eye for detail, develops his techniques of characterization. Sometimes it comes as a surprise to Galindo's reader that he is questioning values which are customarily accepted by bourgeois society. He is not putting Mexico on trial, nor is he even placing humanity in the dock; rather, he invites a review of patterns of behavior that we take for granted, and poses a question as to whether we may not be able to do better.

In 1964, Galindo published his most recent novel, *La comparsa (The Masquers)*. Here he looks into the lives of a cross section of a single city, before and during Carnival. His unifying factor in this novel is time, rather than a narrowly defined group. And the need to reproduce the cross section led the author to some of his most interesting techniques. Awareness of this novel's structure points up Galindo's subtlety as a technician. His fiction is so calmly convincing that one rarely thinks of how he composes it. While some novels cry out for analysis, Galindo's offer themselves quietly and confidently. He moves so skillfully from third-person description to interior monologue, it is doubtful that a casual reader would remember whether he uses interior monologue or not. He joins the three levels of time just as unobtrusively, and changes viewpoint without begging for attention.

As Galindo works on new novels, it is hard to guess what innovations he may use. He thinks of his work as life in growth —a process in which things happen to people because they are —and is not very aware of technique. Mexican fiction of the past three or four years has tended to be stridently innovative. Fuentes' most recent novel, *Cambio de piel (A Change of Skin)*, is a combination of consolidated elements of time and an insistence on the irrationality of life. Fuentes has moved toward a sense of the absurd that is apparent also in a number of younger authors. In some, this attitude—basically negative according to long-accepted values—turns into an ingenuous affirmation of the fact of being. It is quite possible that Galindo would say, if he were questioned, that these novels depart too radically from reality. But there is no doubt that his own novels are unreal according to some standards. In the process of writing, it is unlikely that Galindo will make a prior decision about how innovative he will be. That decision will be made by the novelist's instinct.

For several years prior to 1964, Galindo was director of the press of the University of Veracruz, in Xalapa, the country's most distinguished publishing house outside Mexico City. He was also editor of *La Palabra y El Hombre,* one of Mexico's best reviews. Since that time he has been chief of the section of the Instituto Nacional de Bellas Artes that coordinates cultural activities in the provinces.

THE PRECIPICE

chapter 1

"Yes, it's a gorgeous day," Lorenza said as she fastened the pin of cultured pearls almost at the neckline of her mother-in-law's black wool dress. The piece of jewelry had not been worn by Doña Teresa for seven years. Lorenza continued, "I'm happy for her. My impression the first day was sad because the fog was so heavy you couldn't see more than three feet ahead."

"That's the way it was when my husband brought me, too." She arched her neck and looked at herself in the mirror.

"Pretty?"

"No, misty. Very misty," Doña Teresa replied.

Lorenza studied the living room. Everything was clean and in order. When they stopped talking, there was such a great stillness in the enormous room that they seemed to have ceased existing. Lorenza discovered it was because the clock had stopped at eight o'clock the night before, a little while before she and her husband went to bed. She looked at her wrist watch and set the clock. The tick-tock started lazily, against its will, until it acquired its accustomed rhythm and reintegrated into life everything that was there within.

"It wasn't so bad for us because you and I were accustomed to the mist," Doña Teresa said, alluding to the fact that both of them had been born in Jalapa. She smoothed her gray hair, then continued. "But this poor girl is used to the sun and heat . . . What pretty flowers! Where did you buy them?"

"In town. One of the men went for them."

"The church was full of flowers today. I prayed earnestly for them that God might be gracious to them and make them happy. I have promised to do the 'first Fridays' again."

"I wish you hadn't promised anything. The weather will turn bad later and you won't be able to go."

"I will go, my dear. I will go."

Lorenza went back to the window and looked out again at the road to town. It seemed strange to see it so light, because mist covers the town of Las Vigas almost the whole year—a dense, wet mist that eliminates the sky's distance and makes it descend until it touches the uneven stone paving of the streets. The surroundings—the woods and the gardens—are habitually sunk in dense shadows. There are times, even in the spring, when the town seems to have disappeared, completely hidden from the view of the travelers who go along the highway from Jalapa to Perote. There were not many bright days when they could enjoy the sight of the town hanging on the mountainside and its ring of hills peopled with pine trees.

An opening and closing of doors made Lorenza turn away from her observation post.

"And Gabriel?" Joaquina asked.

"He's bathing," Lorenza said. "He was in the pigsties, two sows had pigs last night. Now there are fifteen more little pigs."

"Fifteen young ones," repeated Joaquina, making rapid calculations. "Not bad. Tell him that the men haven't carried feed to the corral. And he should speak to them about loafing around. We women are loafers enough for everybody."

She went out hurriedly in the direction of the pigsty without caring about her new black silk dress. Lorenza was aware of a pleasant scent. It was unusual for Joaquina to be wearing perfume. She looked at her mother-in-law, who had sat down and crossed her hands. There was nothing to do except wait, so she sat down by her side.

"When we came out of church, I told Father that Hugo was coming back today," Doña Teresa said to her daughter-in-law.

"He was so glad! When I go to Mass tomorrow, I'll invite him to have dinner with us next Sunday."

Lorenza thought about her son. Where could he be? She had seen him leave with one of the maids. Really she didn't have to worry since he was an obedient and cautious child. She had forbidden him to go to the arroyo and he obeyed. Often she had watched from the window of her bedroom as he vacillated about going down the steps and running along the bank of the stream, but generally when he got to the second step he returned, looked for her, and asked her to go with him. Then she would accept happily and together they would take a long walk beside the stream. After that they would play mountain climbing, the two of them scrambling over stones, going up the hill on the steep side. They would go to the stables and to the pigsties and then down the opposite side to the front of the house. When they got there, instead of going in they would run to the back to explore the chicken houses. When the walk ended, they would be happy and frozen. The grand finale was always in front of the fireplace, which Gabriel would hurry to light for them. Now another woman was going to enter this family circle where everything was so right, so complete.

Gabriel, clean, solid, enormous, entered the living room.

"Haven't they got here yet?"

"No. Give me a cigarette."

"Mass today was very solemn. They elevated the Host."

An uncertain sun lighted the arrival of the new Señora Coviella to the town. Hugo slowed down so the automobile wouldn't bump as it entered the turnoff, and Esther had her first view of the place. On her right rose the hills covered with tender grass. On her left the earth ended suddenly and precipitously and the fog began.

"El Bordo is over there where you see the mist."

In front of them, the village, the towers of two churches, and two lines of houses that opened the way. The road was bordered by glistening pines and by apple trees loaded with small green fruit. Hugo accelerated abruptly and Esther looked at him uneasily. Now, in these last moments before arriving at the home of the Coviellas, she would have liked to stop the automobile. She felt a kind of doubt coming alive within her, almost a fear. They entered the town. All the houses had facades with great doorways. Old dusty doorways that in some faraway time had been white, and still, in spite of ill repair, were pleasant and inviting. There were a few men standing in the doorways to the seed stores and grocery stores.

"That's the school. There's the bakery. The doctor lives around the next corner, in the second house. That's the jail and over there is the market place."

There was not enough time for Esther to see where each thing was, so she just nodded without saying anything. They came to the center of town. She saw the church, also white, also dusty and in poor repair, with a small garden in front. Some women dressed in mourning black were walking through the garden, chatting. They stopped talking to look at Hugo and Esther. Hugo greeted them and pronounced five or six names that she did not hear. At the church corner they turned by the side of the park, where several men from the country were talking. Esther didn't really see them but got a general impression of a group of gray sarapes and sombreros. She thought about the park in Cuernavaca, about how different it was from this one. Enormous India laurels grew there and in their shade both tourists and natives took refuge from the heat. In this park there were some rosebushes and one feeble cypress. And the natives (there were no tourists here) had to move away from the shade to keep from getting cold. "Will I come to love this?" she asked herself. She had lived in Mexico City during the first six years of her life and in Cuernavaca the following twenty. But she felt no particular affection for either place.

"The cemetery is just ahead," Hugo explained.

"Now you are the guide," she said, trying unsuccessfully to revive the happiness that had been theirs during the wedding trip. "But I don't think I'm interested."

A few seconds more and the trip would be over forever. Would she be able to keep the memory of those all too brief hours full of happiness and discoveries—contacts—smiles—thinking the same thing at the same time and being able to laugh together? Or would it all disappear the way skin stops tingling once it is used to caresses? More than fearing the breaking of their union, she feared living with other people. Having to divide and share, to fight. "If only there could be a truce," she said to herself. But truces exist only in real battles. In real life there are only brief subterfuges, negations. There can be no truce because there is no battle. Only desire, the desire of uniting blindly with him.

They turned to the left and proceeded slowly along an unpaved street where the houses were humble yet gay. Along the wire fences in front, a climbing vine—in tones from rose to red —lightened the misery of the dwellings. Afterwards they passed an intersection where five roads came together—there the businesses were saloons—and then they kept on for more than a kilometer along a lonely road. When she was about to ask if they would be much longer getting there, the property of the Coviellas appeared, protected by a ring of pine trees.

"There it is," Hugo said.

Above the pines Esther saw the smoke of a chimney against a vaguely blue sky.

"That's the kitchen chimney."

The front of the house was one story, but her husband had already explained to her that since the land fell off toward the back, the inside of the house was really two stories. The front was covered by a flowerless, almost dried-up honeysuckle whose branches wound around each other capriciously. Only the openings corresponding to four windows and the door remained free from the vine. The roof descended on a diagonal, covered by tiles that were green from the dampness. At the top there was a small mirador.

When they got close the dogs began to bark.

"How many dogs do you have?"

"Four, if the bitches haven't whelped recently."

She was pleased by all this. The moment, the house, the pines, the dogs barking. She had always dreamed about a home like this and about being welcomed by dogs who recognized their masters from a distance. She felt that from this moment on she was through with her mother, with the hotel, with the German Meyer.

Before Hugo could park the car the family came out to receive them. Esther responded to the general smile. She already knew two of the four people: her mother-in-law and Aunt Joaquina. They had come to "ask for her" and a month later they had come back for the wedding. With their long dresses of black brocade, both of them had worn enormous Sevillian mantillas that were inappropriate for the insufferable heat of that day in Cuernavaca. Her mother-in-law, who was the color of wax, looked like a melting candle. Her fragility was even more noticeable by the side of Joaquina, who was tall and strong. Both of them were already more than fifty years old, but Joaquina seemed young and had been prettier than her sister-in-law. She was still vigorous and the rosy color of her cheeks was almost the way it had been thirty years before when she came to this country from a village in Asturias. During the wedding the aunt had stared at her as if she were trying to discover what Esther was, what she knew, what she thought. That day after the religious ceremony she came to her to embrace her, and without anyone noticing she handed her a thousand-peso bill. "Just in case Hugo ends up with no money," she said. "It is yours." Esther was so astonished she wasn't able to say no. And Joaquina was right. The last expenses of the wedding trip were paid with the thousand pesos, which Hugo received with an enormous burst of laughter.

"These two you don't know," Hugo said, pointing to his brother and sister-in-law. "This is Gabriel. This is Lorenza."

She embraced all four of them and with a nod she greeted the maids and some field workers who had also come to meet her. The dogs sniffed her for a few seconds and then devoted themselves to making circles around Hugo—four beautiful Dalmatians, happy and rough. Doña Teresa ordered a field worker to shut them up.

"They aren't dangerous?"

"Only at night," Joaquina said.

"Come in," her mother-in-law and Lorenza said at the same time.

In the living room there was cognac, sherry, and a plate of ripe olives on a carved mahogany table. Through the window she saw Hugo speaking with the field hands. There were four of them—solid, dark men looking at her husband affectionately. When Hugo spoke of them, he always called them "the men." He knocked off one of their hats and ran into the house, stopping in the doorway to the living room.

"Where is Eusebio?"

"Here."

Esther saw the owner of the voice. A little boy with the chestnut hair of the Coviellas but with very different features. Enormous eyes in a sad and sensitive little face. "What a beautiful child!" she thought.

"Come and meet your aunt Esther."

"No," the child answered and started to run away, his uncle following him.

Esther looked at her sister-in-law. "Your son is very beautiful!"

"Thank you," Lorenza responded with satisfaction.

Hugo came back to sit beside her and told her that for the moment Eusebio did not want to meet her. Gabriel approached to offer them a drink. Esther looked at him carefully and decided that the physical differences between him and her husband were minimal. She sipped the sherry contentedly and responded to one of her brother-in-law's jokes. Then she let her eyes wander around the living room. It was a tranquil, intimate place. The fireplace was full of logs. She could imagine how the days and nights that awaited her might be. She saw her new family and thought about the hotel table where she used to eat every day with Hans Meyer and her mother. "Sweetie, Hans wants to know if you would rather have something else to eat.

You ought to eat better. Take a little exercise so you'll have a better appetite." "I swim everyday before you two get up." She returned to the present: Hugo was telling the tellable part of the wedding trip. They laughed. The conversation became general and she did not mind answering the questions they asked her.

". . . Well, Mamá, I don't know . . . Maybe she'll come to see us some day. She has so much work at the hotel. Cuernavaca is full of tourists all year long."

"And you used to work with her?"

"Not really. I didn't do much. In the beginning I did, when we first started the business. But later . . ."

"Here you will have to work," Joaquina interrupted.

"Of course. Anyway, it will be good for me to do something." For a moment—largely because of the agreeable effect of the sherry—she was on the point of saying something more, of telling them all, even more than she had told Hugo, but . . . But it was too soon (curious that one cup of sherry would have that effect—undoubtedly a nervous reaction to having to be pleasant, cordial). It would be better for them not to know. Yet the difficulty was not that they might or might not know something. It was the problem of telling that something. What was it exactly? A life—her life—any life could be told in a thousand ways, all different and all true. It all depended on an undetermined point of observation that at times seemed decisive and at times incongruous and false. To speak of herself was to speak of her mother (do I understand her?), of Hans Meyer, of the hotel, of the needlessly intense shades of bougainvillaea that she saw from her window every day, of the tourists, and finally of Hugo.

"Could I have cognac?" she said when Gabriel started to fill her cup.

"Do you smoke?" Lorenza asked, offering her a cigarette.

"No."

"Do you know how to cook?" her mother-in-law asked.

Esther smiled. The tone had been absolutely inoffensive but the question inevitably recalled certain scenes. She (or her mother) in the enormous kitchen of the hotel asking the recent arrival, "Do you know how to cook?" They always answered yes, but none of them knew how. So Tino, the official chef, grumbling but very pleased, kept on deciding what would be prepared that day in the hotel.

"Yes," she answered.

"I'm glad. Some day we will try one of your delicious meals," said Gabriel, who appeared to have guessed her thoughts. He added, "Lorenza is a specialist in desserts: pastries, cookies, custards, anything sweet."

"And he doesn't like desserts," said Lorenza, laughing.

"We will try your cooking tomorrow," said Aunt Joaquina, taking a sip of sherry.

"I hope you like it," Esther replied.

"And if they don't like it, you can tell them to go to the devil and let Mamá keep on cooking," Hugo said as he gave her a kiss. "Cheers to the newlyweds, may they have many children and win the lottery—a million dollar one."

"May God give you a son," said Joaquina. "You can make the million working."

"Not in a million years," said Gabriel. "Cheers."

"Come."

She got up. A chill passed over her as she drew away from the fire. She put her hands on his shoulders and held him a brief moment near the warmth.

He looked for her lips—they had already learned and each time it was better. Yes, the living room was cozy and intimate. A gentle silence broken occasionally by the crackling of the wood. Outside, a lonely night without the noise of people or things. She rubbed against his cheek, along his jaw where the beard was beginning to show.

"Come."

Arms about each other, in the dark, they walked the few steps that separated them from their bedroom. Inside, as a surprise for her, there was another fire.

"Who . . .?" she murmured, a little dizzy from the cognac and kisses. "When?"

"I did. When I left you. It's not so cold for us, but you must be sensitive to it."

"No," she answered, again close to his lips.

Hugo pushed her away gently, took her face between his rough hands, and asked, "Are you pleased?"

But Esther didn't know exactly what he was referring to. The kiss, the day, his family? In order not to make a mistake she said yes. Anyway, fundamentally it was yes to everything. She closed her eyes and let herself be caressed while she felt the warmth of the fireplace on her back. She could look at the bedroom over Hugo's shoulder. Her husband was charming. He knew how to be tender, considerate. He had put her nightgown on this side—the one near the fireplace—so she would have more warmth. Esther thought vaguely about the first white nightgown she had used on their wedding night, about their mutual clumsiness, about his hoarse voice when he told her, "You're the first virgin . . ." The logs crackled. For the first time in her life she had drunk more than she should, but Hugo had insisted. The two of them had stayed with Gabriel and Lorenza in front of the fireplace, chatting, laughing, drinking. The world makes me so happy, so very, very happy! She closed her eyes and opened them again. Suddenly she felt frozen.

"Look at what is over there." Her heart began to pound with a special rhythm that seemed to be telling her something.

Hugo looked, but didn't see anything. The room was in shadow. Quickly he turned on the ceiling light and ran toward his bureau.

"What is it?"

"The pistol, over there."

His first reaction was indignation, but he saw she was pale, trembling, and he burst out laughing.

"This?"

"Yes. Leave it alone. Don't touch it. Who put it there?"

"It's mine. Each of us has one in his room. We live in the country . . ."

His explanation was definite but not harsh. Still, Esther in-

sisted on his getting it out of her sight, so he put it away in the
closet.

An hour later he was asleep. Esther freed herself from his
embrace without withdrawing from his body, and looked at
the coals. Only one log was still burning. Now and then a
briefly intense warmth reached her face. She was tired and
sleep was overcoming her, but now she saw confusedly a scene
from the day. Little Eusebio was running in front of them holding Lorenza's hand. She saw the outside walls of the house—
the side next to the arroyo. They were heavy walls and looked
rather like the side of a church because of their age and solidity.
Then she felt Hugo's hand in hers helping her climb the hill,
and she saw the landscape from up there. She smelled the pines.
She felt the cold air touch her body. When she left the house
Joaquina had stopped her to give her a heavy shawl. "Use this.
It's cold outside. And don't go too far." Her concern seemed
strange after the declaration that she had made halfway
through the meal. "I hope Hugo has explained to you clearly
that everybody here works. Or at least we are all supposed to.
The land and the animals are our work, our life, and it is obvious that the horse gets fat only when he is under the watch-
ful eye of the master." And then including Gabriel and Lorenza,
"Let me tell you something. You don't know what it means to
really work, what it is to have to get up at five o'clock in the
morning or earlier to go out to work in the fields. And I don't
mean rich fields like these where we have people to work them.
No, I mean to be the field workers. You don't know what that
is. Here you are the masters, and everything turns out too easily
for you. You will never know what it is to really work, never."
Following Joaquina's discourse there was a silence that Gabriel broke by saying: "After coffee we will take you to see the
place." Lorenza yawned, and then the voice of Doña Teresa:
"Sunday I will invite Father so you can meet him." On the hill
there were the pigsties and a small stable. Gabriel explained to
her that the rest of the livestock was a kilometer away in a pasture where there were also stables and a caretaker. They intro-

duced the four men, who were drinking, celebrating the fiesta, the marriage. "This is Alejandro, Francisco, Lucio, Cristóbal." She told them all that she was glad to meet them and extended her hand to each one. They walked for more than an hour. The cold became more intense. The afternoon was gray and damp. They all returned to the house on the run. Tired and laughing, Esther stopped at the entrance. Hugo took her in his arms. "I'll fix this," she thought, looking at the honeysuckle on the front of the house. "I'll prune it and then I'll plant some things here in front. It can be a very pretty garden." When they got back the fireplace in the living room was burning. Joaquina was waiting for them.

She heard the dogs barking. The fire was going out. Some of the last, small flames ran like a snake's tongue along the black log and disappeared in a narrow column of smoke. Esther felt cold and snuggled closer to her husband's body. They had gone to bed nude and it made her feel protected and happy.

chapter 2

A gray cat jumped to the top of the fence, balanced himself miraculously, and then advanced without a single misstep until his nose touched Gabriel, who turned around to caress him.

"We'll have to separate them," he exclaimed, disgusted.

He threw his cigarette on the ground and jumped over the fence to where Cristóbal stood.

There were three steps that led up to the highest part of the pigsty fence. Cristóbal went ahead and let himself down inside. Gabriel, erect, with his hands on his belt, looked over the scene. The sow ran to the far end and started making menacing grunts. Cristóbal picked up the two corpses. At the other end, under a small asbestos roof, the siblings of the dead pigs were sleeping, indifferent to crime and to danger. A fine rain began to fall. After an imperceptible moment of repugnance Gabriel stretched out his hand and Cristóbal put the corpses in it. His hand was enormous. One of them could hold both bodies, one on top of the other—what was left of them. Then revulsion overcame him and he threw them away. The cat jumped quickly. He approached cautiously, sniffing. Gabriel wiped his dirty hands on the cloth of his trousers.

"Give me the others."

"Here they are."

Gabriel placed them, two by two, in the other pigsty, where the other new mother looked at them intrigued, surprised. The animal was puzzled, grunting, demanding an explanation. The newborn pigs looked under her.

"There aren't going to be enough teats," Cristóbal said, letting the last one drop. "Those are a lot of mouths for one nurse."

"This place has to be washed carefully, it stinks."

He noticed how Cristóbal started to clean the pigsty with his feet and hands, without objecting to it in the least. Cristóbal was the youngest of the men. His body was hard and muscular. Because he looked like a prize fighter, Hugo was constantly giving him nicknames that were later repeated by his three companions and sometimes by the whole town. He lived with his mistress, a woman older than he, to whom he turned over his salary every Saturday. Gabriel appreciated the obedience and respect of the men because they were sentiments born more of affection than of fear. They had known him since he was a child and they used to speak to him in a familiar fashion. But for seven years now—since the death of Don Eusebio— they had all accepted him as boss and had no longer joked with him the way they had before. He supposed that now they would do the same with Hugo, although surely his brother was not going to stop making jokes with them. Gabriel thought about Esther with satisfaction. Beyond any doubt Lorenza was more beautiful, but Esther had a very special grace, something that came from the ease with which she smiled and from the light in her eyes before she spoke. Last night they had all had a good time together. Perhaps they had drunk more than they should have.

He went to the stable, to the water faucet. He knew that the men nudged each other because he washed twenty times a day. The blood that had spilled down his wrist made him remember the day Eusebio was born. They had planned for him to be born in Jalapa in the house of Lorenza's great-aunt, but he came ahead of time and had to be born here. Lorenza had showed that she had more courage than any of them supposed. No one heard her scream. Her eyes grew large and her face grew pale and red alternately. When the last cry was going to burst from her, the cry of the decisive pain, she fainted. The doctor handed the child to him and Gabriel took it, completely overcome, without seeing it, without wondering whether it was a boy or a girl. His attention was fixed on her, on her breast as it slowly started moving up and down again. Joaquina had to shout to him, "Give him to me, wake up!" in order to make him notice that he held his son in his hands. "It's a boy," Doña Teresa exclaimed, "it's a boy!" "She is all right now," the doctor said. Then Gabriel left the room, weak with a happiness that was very close to weeping. Later Lorenza asked him for the details of what he had seen, but he couldn't tell her. It was inexpressable for him. He had forgotten all the pain, all the horror, just like the mother. That day when he drank a toast with the men, Francisco, laughing, pointed out to him, "Today you didn't wash your hands." "It is my son," he thought.

Now Eusebio was three years old. He was more Landero than Coviella; he would never be a field hand. A few more years of saving and they would be able to live in Jalapa again. With Hugo married and living here (today Hugo had gotten up at six in the morning for the first time in his life and had gone to the stables to get the milk) Gabriel had solved the only problem that kept him from planning to leave Las Vigas. Now his mother and Joaquina would not be alone. Hugo—he knew it well—loved this place, this land, and would stay here forever. Not Gabriel. He wanted to live in the city, to build apartment houses and live on his income. He was thirty years old. And before he was forty he hoped to be well established in Jalapa, and later on to take a trip to Europe. He had never been particularly interested in seeing Villaviciosa, where his father came from; but Lorenza had convinced him that a trip to Asturias was a good excuse for getting to Italy. We will do it, he thought, one day I will take them.

The rain had stopped, and the clarity of the sky suggested that there would be no more. It was June. In a little while, for a few hours, the countryside would be brilliant. The hills and the farm lands would be seen sharply against the horizon. He lit a cigarette. The cat was gnawing at the remains.

"Scat! Leave that for the dogs." Gabriel ran to frighten him away and the cat fled with the speed of an arrow toward the house along a path only he could use, a path he had discovered in his constant flights from the dogs. Gabriel followed his escape, smiling, until he lost him behind the rosebushes. He looked at his watch. It was not yet eight o'clock and the morning work—looking over the corrals, the stable, and the pigsties —had been finished with the help of his brother. He still had no desire to eat breakfast.

"I am going to cut wood," Cristóbal said.

Gabriel stood at the brow of the hill, watching the house emerge gradually from the enveloping mist, and imagined Lorenza still asleep in the gentle warmth of their bedroom.

From a distance he saw Esther climbing the hill carefully.

"Where is Hugo?"

"He went to the pasture."

"He didn't wake me up. Good morning."

"Good morning. Are you an early riser?"

"In Cuernavaca I was. Every day at six. But today the room was very dark and I slept later than I should have."

"It's early. Lorenza and Aunt Joaquina are still asleep."

"Eusebio was already up but he still doesn't want to be my friend. He didn't want to come with me."

"Soon he will love you."

"And where is your mamá?"

"What . . .? In town. At Mass."

The sound of Cristóbal's ax broke the silence just at the right time. As if the noise were some kind of secret sign, they both began to walk side by side toward the stable.

"Which of the men lives there?"

She pointed to a small construction built on to the side of the stable.

"Alejandro. The oldest."

Without hesitating, they followed a path toward the woods, just as if they had planned since last night that they would take a walk at this time. The ground was slippery beneath the pines. It was from there that they saw Cristóbal leaning over the logs. Gabriel led her to a place that looked like a pool because of

its dimensions and depth. They walked beside it in order to descend by a road that was new to her. On the way, Gabriel began to tell her about his first trip to Las Vigas—when he was eleven years old—and how the landscape and even the house itself had seemed enormous, interminable, to him.

He and Hugo used to play getting lost, gleefully supposing that they actually were lost and that suddenly all the grown-ups would begin to look for them everywhere without finding them, until the last happy moment which only they had foreseen.

Esther laughed.

"Didn't you play things like that?"

"Yes," she assured him rapidly. "I used to love getting lost in the hotel by taking the master key and hiding in an empty room. I would get behind the wardrobe or go into the bath-room and wait for Mamá to come weeping to find me. She always found me in a few minutes, but one day I noticed that she never actually found me. Her appearance in the particular room had been a real accident and if it had not been for the necessity of renting it to someone, she might never have come to look for me."

Suddenly she stopped. Why had she told that? Nobody had asked her for intimacies. She was just sharing innocent memories with her brother-in-law. She had the uncomfortable feeling that she had talked too much and so she stopped. But Gabriel didn't seem to notice anything unusual. He acted as if he belonged only to this exact, logical, and simple world of pines, cold, and nature. Now they were walking by the side of a small brook and she had to be very careful because the ground was slippery. Curiously, it was not wet, because the tops of the pine trees had formed a perfect roof for keeping out the rain.

Gabriel started talking again. One day they had crossed the communal farm lands and then had run and run until they actually were lost. They ended up a long way away and a coal miner brought them back on his burro.

Another silence fell over them, but this time she was able to take advantage of it.

"And your father, what was he like? Hugo has told me very little about him."

Gabriel didn't answer right away. He thought and decided that there was no point in telling anything but the truth. Sooner or later someone would tell Esther all about Don Eusebio.

"He was an indecisive, irresponsible man, with blue eyes. Very good but unable to cope with the world. He adored us. He loved everyone and I think everyone loved him a great deal. He also drank a lot."

Esther blushed.

"My father was good, too, nothing exceptional, just an ordinary man. An engineer who worked, built, and left some money for his family. He became ill on a trip to Chiapas, where something bit him. Later gangrene set in and he shot himself. Mamá never told me about his shooting himself but I know it . . ."

They looked at each other. Gabriel understood that it was hard to say what they had said but that each had done it for the sake of the other. Yes, he was fond of his sister-in-law.

Now the house was in sight. Esther was surprised because she had expected to come out at the side of the house rather than at the front. They kept on walking. Finally he said it.

"Do you love Hugo a great deal?"

She was expecting something. She knew that a certain question ought to be asked, but she didn't expect that one.

"Yes," she answered emphatically, feeling insulted.

He perceived her indignation, saw her face redden.

"No," he explained, "what I mean is . . . Hugo needs a lot of love, a great deal."

His disturbed reaction calmed her.

"I know, Gabriel. I know."

chapter 3

"Certainly I can do it!" she repeated to herself once again as she climbed slowly and laboriously but full of joy. Her foot was about to slip into a small hole and she stood for several seconds balancing herself on a loose rock that threatened to throw her into a puddle. She kept on, and repeated to herself what she had told the women of the congregation: "Certainly I can do it!" Stubborn women, she always had to tell them the same thing. A little bit of mud wasn't worth worrying about. It would have been bad if there had been some other kind of danger, but walking didn't expose her to anything. At this hour there never were any drunks, and anyway all the drunks knew her and nobody would have dared to insult her. But the women that day had insisted more than usual.

"You shouldn't go by yourself. The road is bad, you won't be able to do it."

"Certainly I can. God willing, I can do it."

"Wait for my husband to take you."

"No, I can do it alone!"

And they had to stay there at the church door without finding out anything about the new arrival. Doña Teresa was so absent-minded. Some mentioned it now. She was so absent-minded, she had forgotten to invite them. Because she invited Father to dinner on Sunday. If Luchita had heard it, it had to be right, because Luchita hears everything. Doña Teresa heard the comments and pretended to be thinking of something else. The light of the street caused her to blink slightly in spite of the fact that it was not a bright day but a rather dull one. It was raining lightly, and it was a little cold. She began to walk.

A kind of unfathomable joy had filled her ever since she woke up. First she attributed it to the deep sleep that she had enjoyed. She had not slept so peacefully for years. Later—when she was in church—she realized that she owed it to Esther for having freed her from her responsibilities toward Hugo. The image of the altar disappeared before her eyes and in its place appeared Hugo's face with an expression of happiness unknown to any of them. "I met a girl in Cuernavaca. Her name is Esther . . ." Doña Teresa liked to think that the engagement of her younger son was in many respects like her own. Hugo and Esther had met each other in a hotel. She and Eusebio in a boarding house. (Of course, there was one great difference: her engagement had lasted six years, Esther's engagement less than six months.) Eusebio Coviella was a newcomer to the country. She was the one that opened the door for him the first day he came, then ran to call to her mother: "It's a Spaniard who's looking for room and board." Eusebio was at that time a young man of seventeen and his eyes were the bluest that Teresa had ever seen. They were the same age. They talked a lot. They soon became friends and she offered to mend his clothing for him the day she found him doing it himself. Eusebio broke with two of the customs of the Spaniards who were already established in the city: he didn't devote himself to making money at whatever personal cost, and in spite of his uncertain economic situation he became the sweetheart of a poor Mexican girl. The Spanish Colony immediately disapproved of his attitude. The elders called him to offer advice; others made fun of him. But Eusebio was not offended easily and he didn't pay much attention to what was happening around him. It might be better to say that he didn't notice it, that he dreamed about something very distant and very much his own and that within this dream there was space only for the presence of Teresa. His countrymen who had had him brought over so that he could help in the business dismissed him one fine day without much explanation. Finding another job was not easy. The Spanish Colony intervened again. They offered to return him to Spain. Eusebio shook his head negatively, and came a little closer to reality. He had no reason at all for wanting to go back to Villaviciosa. He had too many brothers, sisters, cousins, and uncles, and there was not enough land for all of them. They were poor and they had to work too much and too hard to obtain what was absolutely necessary. Sending him to America had been a commercial failure but at least he would not return to become a burden again, to add one more mouth. Again he sought the aid of his countrymen, and it was a Basque, Luis Larragoitia, who helped him out of his difficulties and became his friend. Larragoitia had innumerable business ventures. He was the richest of the local Spaniards—indeed, the richest in several neighboring cities—and he thought so much of Eusebio that he placed him where he would not have to do anything important or tiring. His protector had been in the country for twenty years. He was a bachelor and one night he confessed that he wanted to go to look for a wife in Asturias because his mother had been from that province. In a letter to his parents Eusebio wrote that his boss was coming there and that he was going to marry a girl from that region. Some six months after Luis Larragoitia left, it became known in the city that he was married. Eusebio heard the news with a smile. Two weeks later he received a letter from his home town. He ran downstairs to find Teresa and tell her, "Listen, who do you think Larragoitia married? My sister Joaquina. I didn't think she was that clever."

That night Eusebio told her more about his family. He came down to the living room with the photos he had brought with him. Joaquina was in one of them, pretty, rustic, unpolished. He told her that his father and Joaquina quarreled every day, that they almost hated each other, and that undoubtedly Joaquina had married Larragoitia in order to get away from her father. It was the first she knew about her sister-in-law. At the end of that year Eusebio insisted that she had to go with him to Veracruz to wait for them at the pier. Contrary to everything they expected of her, Joaquina got off the boat perfectly attired. After living in New York for six months, she dressed in the latest fashion. It was her brother who was most astonished by her appearance.

The following year, and without telling anyone until the last moment, Eusebio and Teresa were married. It was the fall of 1926. Religion was outlawed. A distant relative of Teresa took it upon herself to find a priest, who married them in the little living room of the boarding house under the severe scrutiny— almost disapproving—of Joaquina. A few months later Luis Larragoitia died of a heart attack.

"My Eusebio also died of a heart attack. I am sure that his heart failed him," she said to herself. She almost whispered it as she knelt automatically, brought back to reality by the sound of the bells that the sacristan was ringing. Weddings, births, deaths: that is life, she thought. Work and hard times were years behind. She would dedicate today's communion to Hugo and Esther and would ask God to give them a child soon. That would complete the stabilization of her boy.

The rain had stopped. She came to a halt and dried her face with a tiny handkerchief. She sneezed, then continued her journey, caressing the handkerchief between her fingers. It was a gift from Lorenza. "It is Swiss," she had said when she gave it to her. Lorenza's gifts were always fine, delicate. She reflected that she seldom thought about her and Gabriel. The fact is, they never worry me, she explained to herself, sneezing again. She identified them with a feeling of exactness and moderation. And little Eusebio (it's a pity he didn't inherit his grandfather's eyes) produced the same effect. It pleased her that her grandson was that way—unquestionably a Landero. That is to say, a member of one of the oldest families of Jalapa. One of the few that could be considered aristocratic. A family that was known since before the French Intervention. Eusebio would have been agreeably surprised to know that four years after his death his oldest son would marry a Landero. It was obvious that the Coviellas' money had been an important factor in Lorenza's decision, but Lorenza was a lady and she had ended up truly loving her husband.

She thought about Esther again. The problem that had harrassed Doña Teresa recently—"What is that girl like?"—had disappeared from her thoughts. She was at peace.

Although closer to Gabriel in opinions and attitudes (because in fact she and he were in agreement on everything), she felt more attached to her younger son. A continuous thread of worries tied her closely to Hugo. Ever since he was small he had been too restless, and she had always worried about him, feeling certain that some danger was lying in wait. Once a fractured ankle when he fell out of a tree. Another time the call from the Red Cross saying that he was wounded—a fight with rocks—then on another occasion that jump right in front of her eyes. Joaquina had ordered him to do something and he refused to obey. "Do it or I'll whip you," Joaquina said as she put out her hand to get a leather belt that was within reach. But before she could get it Hugo ran toward her and buried his teeth in her hand. Joaquina cried with surprise, rage, and pain. With her left hand she hit Hugo on the head until he let her go. She managed to get out of his way and looked around for something to hit him with. He understood her intentions and ran toward the roof garden (they were living in Jalapa then). Generally Teresa did not react rapidly, but that day she ran after him so that it would be she and not Joaquina who would punish him. Everything happened too fast. When she got there Hugo was beginning to climb the wall. "If you come near I'll jump." Teresa hesitated a couple of seconds at most. The height was almost ten feet. Behind her she heard Joaquina coming upstairs. She ran toward him shouting, "No! No!" Then Hugo jumped and Teresa stood stock-still halfway there with her hands immobilized, her arms extended toward where her son had been. It was Joaquina who looked over the wall first, her eyes as wide open as they could be and her cheeks colorless. She saw him get up and run limping toward the street. In tears and anguish they looked for him. They notified their friends as well as the police, but they did not find him. Three days later he came home, and nobody said a word about what had happened.

When she got to the fence of pines Doña Teresa was certain that she had forgotten something. Forgotten or lost? What? She bit her lip and contemplated the rapid breaking up of clouds and mist that the wind pushed away, leaving the sky clean and blue. She had stopped, a little tired, to sneeze again. I've caught a cold. I should have told Gabriel to wait for me in town. What terrible weather! And it's spring already. What was it I forgot? I think maybe . . . I didn't pray my Pater Noster on the way. Funny, I didn't speak to anyone while I was walking. Maybe it was on account of the rain . . . And she decided that that was what it was. The rain had made her walk with her eyes on the ground, and of course also on account of the rain there wouldn't be anyone in the streets. "I know!" she told herself jubilantly. "It was because I'm happy. I slept well and will sleep well from today on. That girl is a charm. She's prettier than Lorenza. No. Yes . . . No, Lorenza is more . . . They are very different. Like Joaquina and me."

She continued on her way, praying the Pater Noster, a little ashamed of her forgetfulness. She hadn't promised it to a saint but to Eusebio, since the day of the Mass of the Novena. "I will go to Mass every day and on the way back I will say a Pater Noster for you." On the days when she couldn't go to church on account of the bad weather, she prayed in the kitchen; and sometimes when she did it aloud without realizing it, Rita the maid—who was completely devoid of imagination—would accompany her.

"Amen," she murmured with her dry lips.

Behind her sounded the engine and horn of the truck as it came noisily and rapidly toward her. She stood close to the bed of tulips and saw Hugo at the wheel.

"Good morning, Sister," he shouted as he passed within inches of her.

Behind on the uncovered truck bed three of the men were

riding, clutching the railings. They also said good morning to her and Teresa answered, smiling at all of them. Hugo could be charming when he wanted to be. He still had the same adorable smile he had when he was a baby. On days like this—days when he smiled that way—he would pick her up and take a few steps of a waltz, swinging her in the air.

From the other direction, before she got to the house and a little after she stopped hearing the engine of the truck, Esther and Gabriel appeared. They stopped to wait for her.

"Esther has been the nurse," Gabriel said.

"What? How? What happened?"

"One of the workmen," she said, shrugging her shoulders to indicate that it was nothing important. Neither what she did nor the accident itself.

"Cristóbal cut his hand while he was chopping wood," Gabriel explained, "but she took care of it very well."

"I'm going to catch up with Hugo," Esther said, leaving them. Doña Teresa watched her walk away. She had changed her tailored suit of the day before for a gray skirt and a coral sweater. Again she thought about herself and Eusebio.

"I like her," she said to Gabriel. She sneezed several times. "She is so . . ."

"Come in, come in. It's cold outside."

"Cold?" Joaquina repeated, frowning, as she went into the kitchen. "On such a clear day . . ."

"You got up late," Gabriel said. "It was misty and it drizzled a little."

"I think I caught a cold."

"Ah," Joaquina responded, gesticulating before telling the news. "Lorenza made breakfast."

"Lorenza?" Gabriel asked, surprised.

She appeared in the dining room door.

"Yes. I want to impress Esther. There are eggs with bacon for everyone."

"Not for me," said Eusebio, shaking his head. "I don't want that, Mamá."

chapter 4

Hugo felt his testicles absent-mindedly.

"What's the matter?" Lucio asked, trying to keep from laughing. "Are they working a lot?"

The men burst out laughing. He was lying on the grass. He turned over half way and stayed face down.

"Oh, shut up, Indian scum. Get to work!"

He looked at the grass: an ant—several—then the legs of the men close to the fence that they were repairing. Alejandro mixed the mortar, spit in it, looked at the sky to see what time it was. Lucio and Cristóbal, standing on the fence, one at each of the sections under repair, made another joke—this time to Francisco, who was carrying the stones. Once in a while someone began to sing and the others joined in on the chorus. Hugo also looked at the gray-blue sky, cut by an occasional bird. They had had almost a week of good weather without a drop of rain and not very much fog. In the afternoon after dinner he and Esther would go to the city. He would take her to the movies and to supper. He looked at the men again.

"Get a move on, you loafers."

"Listen to the boss," Francisco commented, shrugging his shoulders.

"It's one o'clock already," Alejandro said.

"Okay, then," Hugo shouted, jumping to his feet. "Let's have a drink, you sons-of-bitches."

"Don't give Cristóbal anything. He's been goofing off all morning. For a week now he's been complaining about his hand and it doesn't get any better."

"Because the boss's wife is taking care of him," Lucio said.

Cristóbal's eyes darkened, but Lucio didn't notice it. They put the tools aside and began to walk behind Hugo toward Alejandro's house. Alejandro ran ahead so he could get there first and open the door. Cristóbal controlled himself, kicked a rock, and went along with them, smiling all the while. The room —next to Alejandro's living quarters—was a small warehouse where they kept corn, bran, and tools. Hugo had his bar there. On a rough, homemade shelf he had placed some glasses and bottles. Usually only one out of the whole collection contained any liquid. The rest were primarily decorative, although they did serve to evoke memories. There was a cognac bottle, Hugo's wedding gift from the men. They gave it to him wrapped in tissue paper and tied with a red cellophane bow. "Cognac, eh?" he exclaimed, pleased and gratified. "You've been stealing enough from us recently. You probably paid for this with those hens that were missing a few days ago." They laughed happily and then with a certain timidity brought out the other gifts. "This is for the missus," said Alejandro, "because I guess she doesn't drink." "It's a tablecloth," Lucio offered enthusiastically. "My old lady made it. But all of us bought the cloth and thread together." Hugo looked at them. He could easily have wept. "Wait a minute," he said, leaving hurriedly. I won't be long." He came back with Esther. "Now give it to her." The men were uneasy, didn't know what to do. They laughed, they blushed, and they nudged each other. "You speak." "No, you do it." Cristóbal took it, trying not to get dirt on it. "It is for you—a gift from us." "Well, open the bottle, you stupid lout. She's going to take a drink with us. To your health." That's why that bottle would stay there for a long time, perhaps forever. It was a proof that the boss was their friend and was fond of them.

"Cheers."

"To your health!" they said in chorus.

They all emptied their glasses with one swallow and Hugo served seconds.

Looking out from the mirador, Joaquina said bitterly, "They're drinking already."

"Well, it's one o'clock," Gabriel said in the same tone, holding a glass in his hands. "Leave them alone."

"That's right. They stop working right on the stroke of one. Hugo will never be a boss."

"Don't start fussing with him, Joaquina, for God's sake. Don't start. We're all so happy. I'm sleeping well . . . the girl is so good . . . a superb cook. It's obvious she likes us, and he's never been so happy and peaceful in his whole life."

"I know it, I know it, I'm not going to quarrel with him."

"They're going to Jalapa this afternoon," Gabriel said. "I told them they could use the car whenever they wanted to."

"All right. I haven't said anything against it. And I already knew it. She told me. What bothers me is, why do they drink? Why?"

"He didn't steal it," Doña Teresa said.

Joaquina looked at her with a scornful expression.

"Yes. He gets it from the Coviellas, from his father and his grandfather . . . Because according to what you've told us, I gather there aren't any drunks in your family."

"You can ask about my father in Jalapa. Everyone knew him. But if my father had been a drunkard, he wouldn't have run around talking about it. And if my husband drank a lot, that doesn't mean he was bad. Absolutely not! God knows it."

Lorenza struck a match furiously.

"Give me a drink, dear," she said, lighting her cigarette. "And give your mamá and your aunt some sherry. Shall we call Esther?"

"Esther," Joaquina shouted, "come have a drink."

"A storm is coming," Francisco said.

They all looked out to see the sky, still holding their glasses.

The sky was leaden above the pines, which were now dark green. The cornfields suddenly became opaque and blended into the black of the hills.

"If it rains hard, it's going to flood the hut and that kid of ours has a fever," Francisco said, thinking about the youngest of his children, Cheo, a rather sickly boy.

"The water isn't going to come in here," Alejandro commented. "In three years only a few drops have come in just once. I put a little cement there and that took care of it."

"It's not going to rain until after five," Hugo said, and he thought that by that time he would be in Jalapa, in the theater. Then he wouldn't care whether it rained or not.

"If it's not too hard, it would do the flowers a lot of good," Lucio said, because his wife had a garden, where she cut flowers every Wednesday to sell in town. She brought in a lot of money.

Cristóbal didn't worry. When it rained a lot he had an excuse to spend the night at Alejandro's. He was tired of his woman. He didn't love her any more. Every time she demanded something of him, he saw more clearly how old and how ugly she was. "You're tied to her apron strings," Alejandro told him when they talked together about personal matters.

Alejandro went to his room, where there was a brazier that he used for heating his dinner. He looked at the soup. It was smoking. It smelled good.

He went back.

"Shall we have another drink, Boss?"

"Sure."

Francisco took his glass away.

"Boss, I would like to go . . . If it's all right."

"Go ahead. Run."

"A taco," Lucio said.

"There . . . with her," Francisco answered, already on his way.

Every day they brought their dinner to share it with Alejandro, who didn't have anyone to cook for him. Alejandro was old. He was not from this town but had come here from some other place. Years ago somebody had said that he killed a man on the coast and they never knew whether it was true or not. He was a good worker and no one could accuse him of anything except perhaps of drinking too much every Sunday. On Sundays he ate in the house with his bosses. That is, he ate in the kitchen with Rita, who would give him as many beers as he asked for. They laughed a lot together and sometimes—when there were guests—Doña Teresa had to come and tell them to be quiet.

"We're going to finish the fence even if it does rain," Lucio said.

"Right," Alejandro said, "so Doña Joaquina won't get mad."

"And even though nobody would dare mess around here where there's so many dogs," Cristóbal added.

"I know, I know," Hugo said. The night before, Esther had awakened him: "Hugo. Hugo! The dogs are barking a lot. Something is happening." "Go to sleep. You're nervous. They're always barking." In the morning Joaquina discovered the theft: twelve turkeys. The explanation was simple: one of the maids —or perhaps Alejandro—had left the back gate open. There were always thieves around. A lot of them hung around town to see what they could get away with. But Joaquina needed to blame someone closer and known to her. She quarreled with the men and with her nephews about the piece of fence that had fallen down three months before and that nobody had repaired.

"The thief knows his way around here," said Cristóbal. "The house . . ."

"It was probably someone from the collective farm," Lucio said.

"Not one of them," Hugo said. "They aren't thieves."

Lucio was muttering to himself. He had a quarrel with one of the men from the collective farm. He didn't like them and he never missed a chance to say something against them.

"There's a lot of them, Boss. You know how it is."

"Okay, here's to your health. I'm on my way to Jalapa."

Hugo kissed Joaquina when he came in. It was a spontaneous and unusual thing. Joaquina, surprised, responded with good measure, kissing him on both cheeks. The exchange completely altered the atmosphere, which had been oppressing everyone. Suddenly all of them felt a certain relaxation. They went into the dining room with a kind of weariness that reflected their relief. They had been discussing whether Hugo was meeting his obligations or not. Esther had kept quiet. Doña Teresa, Gabriel, and Lorenza had defended Hugo, and Joaquina took the opposite point of view. Now, as she unfolded her napkin, Joaquina smiled, and with her smile conceded that they were right. Of course Hugo works. Certainly he does. This morning he got up before six. He did everything that Gabriel was supposed to do and so Gabriel was able to help her untangle the accounts at her desk. Those detestable books of assets and liabilities, those so-many percents that she had never known how to figure out rapidly in spite of the fact that for thirty-one years—since the death of Luis Larragoitia—she had been in charge of it all.

Hugo (it always happened to him after the third drink) was radiating youth and good humor. Unaware of the argument that had preceded his arrival, he played the clown.

"But the best part was his expression when he tried to cover up his faux pas. Did you notice?"

He reproduced the expression that Father Miguel had had the Sunday before and they all laughed heartily. Everybody felt happy. Doña Teresa chastised herself for being happy. He was openly making fun of the padre and that was not Christian, nor was it pious. But she saw her son and she laughed again until she started to cough.

"Now, son, please, you are going to make me choke."

"And then he threw down his napkin—I insist he threw it down, it didn't just fall—so he'd have a good excuse to see Esther's legs."

The laughter produced by this comment was somewhat less

hearty, but he recreated the moment in pantomime, and before their eyes appeared a Father Miguel who was laughable, clownish, so irrationally authentic and identical to the original that Rita, wondering what they were laughing about, looked in from the kitchen, laughing without knowing why.

Hugh took advantage of the moment to ask her to bring another bottle of red wine. The fact in itself—asking her to bring another bottle to the table—was not at all strange, but the fact that Hugo did it was something new. It was the first time in his life that he had dared to order it, and it didn't occur to anybody that it was out of place. Rita brought it right away.

"There was a fellow in Asturias," Joaquina began, "but I think he wasn't Asturian, maybe he was Galician . . ."

Esther took some cheese. She was beginning to like strong cheeses. She felt satisfied. The sip of wine tasted better on her lips. This had been beyond any doubt the happiest dinner since her arrival. Laughter had not only united them but had managed to wipe away the bitterness and—how strange!—to make her feel more one of them, a part of the family. Perhaps the reason for this feeling was that she had decided not to tell Hugo what had been said before he got there. While she was listening to Joaquina accuse and discourse against her husband, she did not dare judge her. She avoided allowing her thought to arrive at a "She is thus and so," which once formulated (although only mentally) might become irrevocable. It was the same reaction of not wanting to know, of being blind, that governed her relationship with Hans Meyer, until one day, in a decisive way, she came upon the exact words to define him and detest him. She took another sip of wine and looked at Joaquina: her lips were moving rapidly, pronouncing with wonderful clarity the c's, the s's, and the z's. Now she was telling something about a lady from Jalapa. In less than an hour she (Esther) would see that city. She would buy something before going to the movie: flower seeds. Hugo had approved her garden project. In a few months she would change the front of the house. She would ask one of the men to help her prune the

ivy and clean up the ground. What picture are we going to see?

"Cheers," Lorenza said.

She raised her cup. She was standing by the window and could see a streak of lightning tear the heavens at some very distant point. The expected sound never came. Her childhood fears, now gone, had been closely related to storms, skyrocket explosions, and stories about the world coming to an end in a collision of planets. Anything associated with an intense sound terrified her. Self-analysis had convinced her that her fear began one fifteenth of September when a servant had taken her to the Independence Day celebration. Suddenly the rockets began to explode, thousands of fireworks went off. Horrified, she let go of the hand that was leading her and started running, uttering cries that nobody heard, surrounded by bodies, by legs, trying in vain to find an exit or a place to hide. The servant found her in less than five minutes, but Lorenza felt that she had been lost for years, all of them full of mysterious explosions and laughter and incomprehensible movements. She still had a horror of crowds, of confusion, of Independence Day. But noise had stopped bothering her. The piano cured me of that, she said ironically. It is one way to master noise—you can create and *be* noise. One afternoon when she was playing— with lots of mistakes—a concerto by Franck, Esther had opened the door and looked at her with an astonished glance that amused her. "You play the piano?" she asked foolishly. Lorenza stopped playing, stood up, and showed her *her* living room. "I came in because I was fascinated, and I liked what you were playing," Esther explained, a little upset because she had entered a place where she had not been invited. Lorenza laughed. "I play the piano and I have all—almost all—the virtues of ladies of good breeding. The only thing I lacked was money. That's why I married Gabriel." Esther answered with a laugh to show that she took it all as a joke, and now, in this moment, Lorenza admitted to herself that her joke had been out of place and that it was extremely vulgar to say such things to her sister-in-law, who was still almost a stranger. What must Esther have thought? She reproached herself constantly for saying personal things when she shouldn't—things which often were really lies or extremely distorted truths. To a certain extent it was an effective weapon that she had used to disconcert Joaquina or even to shut her up. But when she used the same technique with her mother-in-law, she could never avoid the bothersome feeling that she was taking advantage of her. She felt that she made Doña Teresa think ill of her and that thinking ill would cause Doña Teresa remorse and bring on another confession to the priest. She had never played her little game with Gabriel because she knew that the second time she did it she would get exactly the response she deserved but didn't want. She saw another flash of lightning, and this time she heard the thunder.

"Come on," Hugo said. "Get ready so we can leave before it rains."

"All right," Esther answered, standing up.

At that moment Rita came in with coffee. Joaquina was the first to serve herself. She kept her eyes on Esther and remembered that when she herself was that age she was never able to go out. She was the oldest of the daughters and had been the family's servant girl from the time she was eleven years old. She had to wait on her uncle, her cousins, and her brothers. Before six o'clock in the morning she was up to serve breakfast, and her work never ended. But she could put up with all of it except her father's eyes in the evening—that flushed, absent, repugnant look. She hated even his voice, his drunken orders and songs. She would look at him from the darkness of the kitchen and it comforted her to think that he was despicable, unjust, and vicious. When she would carve a pig, she used to think that her father must have an equal amount of grease in his double chin, in his bloated, alcoholic's cheeks. She detested him, and she might well have killed him one day if that letter had not come from Eusebio: "My employer is going to Asturias. He wants to marry a girl from Asturias because his mother was from there. He will come to visit you." Joaquina looked at herself in the mirror, invented a smile. She could be pretty. Her savings were pitifully small, but she managed to get a loan and went to Gijón to buy herself a dress, some shoes, and a handbag.

Several months passed and one day a tiny nephew shouted the news: "Here is a gentleman from America who knows Eusebio." Joaquina flew to her bedroom, washed her face, and dressed hurriedly. Those were the days when she didn't even think about numbers, and it never occurred to her that Luis Larragoitia was a very rich man. It didn't matter to her whether he was rich or poor. What she needed was someone who would fall in love with her and take her away from there. Someone who would take her to America, far, far away, so she would never see her hateful family again. On the ship, Luis devoted himself to teaching her how to sit down, what to eat, what clothes to wear. She learned how to meet people and make friends with them, and she also learned that she shouldn't say a word in her Asturian dialect. They spent six months in New York and when she got to Mexico she was speaking more correctly than her brother Eusebio. She even had the bearing of a great lady, and she smiled and her eyes lit up when she thought of the clothing that her husband had bought her in New York. But her role of The Lady was brief. After Luis's death it had no meaning. She did not go back to her folkways, but she was no longer interested in being a distinguished person. And now, as the years passed, she felt that she was inevitably becoming a reproduction of her father—his movements, his tone of voice, his acts, everything. It was an inner similarity that showed in spite of her own will; and at the same time her husband, although his memory was tangible in everything that she possessed—in the table, in the wine, in the house—was not even a ghost, and often it seemed that he had never existed. He had left her things, objects, but no emotions. And yet she had indeed loved him. Yes. But it was so long ago . . . so long . . .

"It's going to rain any minute," Hugo said. "We'll be back around ten o'clock."

Joaquina was surprised to see him so carefully dressed. Wearing a suit and a tie, he was very handsome. Lorenza and Gabriel were playing with Eusebio, and Teresa had fallen asleep.

chapter 5

Burgos, the oldest of the Dalmatians, followed Lorenza into Eusebio's little bedroom. He went near the bed and watched her put the child on the bed and then wrap his legs with a shawl.

"Go away, Burgos," she whispered. "He's going to sleep a while. Don't wake him up."

The dog wagged his tail and started following her again. He was the most cherished of the dogs, the only one they permitted to come into the house. Whenever he was freed from his chain he ran to the house looking for the boy. Today he had spent more than two hours going from one place to another without finding him. He began to bark when he heard the automobile approaching, and he was the first to go out to greet Eusebio. But Eusebio was in his mother's arms and he couldn't sniff him.

In one end of Lorenza's living room there was a writing desk. Burgos stretched himself out there at his mistress's feet and looked at her for a few seconds, waiting to be petted or perhaps expecting a reprimand and an order to go out. But she was busy looking in the drawers of the desk and paid no attention to him. Burgos laid his head on the carpet and went to sleep.

The last bank deposit recorded in her passbook was for four thousand five hundred pesos. Lorenza found the checkbook and looked at the balance. Then she began figuring on the back of an envelope. Putting together her savings account and Gabriel's checking account, they had sixty two thousand pesos—a fourth of what she needed. She threw the papers in the drawer and lit a cigarette. Then she looked around the room. She would have a lot more money, she said to herself, a lot more money, if she sold all these things. But she knew that she could never bring herself to do it. Her living room was full of antiques that she had started buying when she was married. They were things intended to go into the Landero house because one day (she promised herself even before she was married) that house would be hers again. Her grandfather, Don Luis Landero, had to sell it in 1915. He was bankrupt and had four young and useless children: Luis, Amelia, Ernesto, and Lorenza. Luis died while he was in Mexico City during the Revolution, spending all that he had gotten out of the sale. Ernesto and Amelia stayed in Jalapa taking care of Don Luis during his last days while the first Lorenza went abroad. "She met an Englishman and they said that he was going to marry her," Aunt Amelia told her one afternoon. "I never believed it but she did. The ship from New York never got to England. Poor dear!" After the death of Don Luis, Ernesto went to work for Don Erasmo Ponce, a seventy-year-old friend of his father who owned several orange and coffee plantations, and he married the old man's only daughter, Eugenia, in 1924. Aunt Amelia always told the second Lorenza, "I preferred to leave the city. I went with some friends of mine to Puebla and met my husband there. He was rather ordinary, but he was rich. And since we were used to eating and dressing well, I had no intention of marrying a poor man. But I'll tell you this, I never gave the people of Jalapa the pleasure of meeting my husband. We lived very much to ourselves so I would be the only one to know about his lack of refinement. And now you see that I'm back here, in my place again, with money. And he is dead and buried. He was a good man with a certain amount of charm. You must remember him . . ." But Lorenza didn't remember him exactly. "They named you Lorenza in honor of your aunt. And to be perfectly frank, we were all somewhat disappointed that you turned out to be a girl. Your parents and

I, all of us, wanted you to be a boy, another Landero, someone who could regain what we had lost."

She had heard this story since she was fifteen years old, and she would ask herself, stretched out on her bed dreaming about being rich, "How much money will it take?" She was familiar only with the front of the house: seven windows, an enormous entry, a wide French-style corridor that led to a garden full of flowers. And the things Aunt Amelia used to point out: "That's the window to your father's room, that one belongs to your grandfather's room, the living room is over there, these three windows . . . The dining room is immense . . ."

And today, after asking herself that same question for fifteen years, she had learned the answer: two hundred and fifty thousand pesos. A quarter of a million. Aunt Amelia had told her. Lorenza shook her head, overcome by the figure. She looked at her aunt—elegant, erect, powerful—and was hopeful.

"You buy it, Aunt Amelia," she exclaimed.

Aunt Amelia smiled.

"But child, what would I do with it? I have enough money to live decently, and if I don't live forever, I will have everything I need. But if I sell all I own to acquire that white elephant, what am I going to do then? Can I eat memories? That house needs furniture, nicknacks, servants, attention." She sighed. "I'm not a millionaire, I would have to turn it into a guest house, or a hotel. Can you imagine? I couldn't live there unless I could do it the way my grandmother and great grandmother did, with a dozen servants and two coaches. It's out of the question, my dear. If I bought it, I would be as poverty stricken as my own mother. Never."

Lorenza made no further efforts to convince her. Instead she began to make mental calculations. How much did she and Gabriel have in cash? A few minutes later the maid came in to tell her that her brother-in-law was waiting for her in the car, and that little Eusebio was already with him. Lorenza kissed her aunt and ran down the stairs. She needed a quarter of a million pesos. She had to get them. The ride to Las Vigas seemed very short and when they got there she noticed that Eusebio had fallen asleep. She took him in her arms and went in to put him to bed.

"My jewelry," she thought. "I could sell it . . ." She stared at Burgos' black and white spots. Then she shook her head. No, Gabriel would never agree to it. The most valuable piece she had was an emerald necklace (How much? Twenty thousand? Twenty-five thousand? Perhaps more?) that he had given her when Eusebio was born. "Our land . . ." She bit her fingernails. "Not that either. He won't want to."

The door opened.

Gabriel came in.

"Hi, how did it go?"

He came over to kiss her. Lorenza took the cigarette from her lips.

"Fine. Eusebio is asleep."

"And how is your aunt?"

"Her rheumatism is bothering her. She sent you her greetings. And she started me figuring."

"About what?"

"They are selling the house." She watched him sit down on the sofa and then she sat down beside him. "My house. Two hundred and fifty thousand."

"Too much."

"We have sixty-two in the bank already," she observed. "We could get more. We could sell something . . . a piece of land . . . the piece near the stadium . . . the piece near the station." Her lips trembled.

Gabriel patted her hand and began to explain to her carefully why they couldn't do any of those things. To sell at this time would be a little like giving it away, actually taking a loss. On the other hand, if they waited five or ten years, they would make a good profit. The cost of property was increasing. Jalapa was growing. What they owned at that time would, as a matter of fact, sell for enough to buy the house. But if they bought it, that money would stop producing. And to make matters worse, the house would bring with it expenses that they would not be able to meet.

"It's just a question of time, of waiting a few more years."

"But I want that house for Eusebio. I want him to grow up there, in his place, in his house."

"I want it, too," he said, frowning.

"In two years we will have to go to live in town. The child can't just stay here. He needs to go to school, to have friends . . ."

"And to have money," Gabriel finished.

"But you promised me," she cried. "That's why . . ."

"That's why you married me?"

Lorenza blushed.

"No. That's why I love you so much. Because when I told you what it meant to me, you understood. It's true that there was a time when that house was the only thing that mattered to me. I told you that for years and years it was my dream, my reason for being. But when I married you, I did it because you had come to be the most important thing for me. And if I've gone back to an early idea it's because of my son and on account of the hopes you encouraged."

"I repeat that one day I'm going to buy it for you."

The door opened suddenly and Hugo's happy face appeared.

"You quarreling?" he asked. "I'm going to call Esther because she thinks that you two never fight."

"No," said Lorenza.

"Yes. No," exclaimed Gabriel. "No."

"Get together on your story and come on upstairs to eat. We're waiting for you."

Hugo made a wry face and went out.

Gabriel went over and kissed her.

"There is another solution," said Lorenza.

"What is it?"

"Joaquina. Could she lend us the money?"

"But darling," he said, caressing her, "you know perfectly well that Aunt Joaquina would never give us money for an investment like that. She has worked too hard to accumulate her money to let it go so easily. Come on, now, let's go. It's time for dinner."

"Papá," shouted Eusebio.

Burgos was the first one to get to the child.

"A lie," Lorenza said to herself. "I need a lie to convince her."

She had drunk too much and now she felt herself in a happy state where she could overcome all the obstacles to the purchase of the house. It seemed to her that her success was imminent in spite of the enormous price. She felt foolish. It seemed so easy to convince, to deceive Joaquina. In the first place, Joaquina adored Eusebio. She was spoiling him all the time and granting him every wish. Why not this one? Why not give her great nephew this enviable place which was appropriate to his heritage and which he deserved? There is a way, there must be a way to convince her. By lying, an ancient and honorable custom . . . She turned to Esther and said. "Do you know that I've lied all my life?"

Esther looked at her. The weak rays of the afternoon sun fell across them.

"You're so strange," she said finally.

"Don't you believe me?" And Lorenza shook her black hair as if she were dancing, as if she were a child.

"It seems to me that . . . I don't know. Do you want to frighten me, Lorenza? Are you trying to impress me?"

"No," she answered, suddenly serious. "Certainly not. Excuse me. I drank too much."

"Not as much as Hugo," Esther said, talking almost to herself.

"I have to deceive Joaquina," whispered Lorenza in the same tone.

Esther, troubled, answered, "What is this all about? Are you trying to test me? Do you want to make me your accomplice?"

But Lorenza did not hear her. Mechanically she lit a cigarette, her eyes lost in the distance, seeing something very different from the green hills before her in the afternoon, very different from the men from the communal farm who were cleaning their cornfield.

Lorenza had told it all to Gabriel. One night several months after they were married. She began the confession with a question.

"Do you remember that dance in elementary school, at the end of the session, when we were in the sixth grade?"

Gabriel smiled that special smile that was so very much his own, yet at the same time so very like Hugo's and so very like Joaquina's.

"Yes," he answered.

"Do you remember the practices in the auditorium? It was like playing grown-ups—a dance, a date. We were all very proud and happy. We were going to dance, to wear long dresses, with our lips and cheeks painted, and you boys were going to wear your black suits and neckties.

"Yes," Gabriel said, "I had a hard time learning the steps."

"You were my date," she interrupted. "A lot of times, later on, I asked myself why were we together? Who decided it? What teacher? What chance?"

"We were a good pair even then," Gabriel said, joking.

"Maybe so, maybe we were a pair of attractive children who thought they were already grown-ups. But there never was a dance. You remember? I mean you and I didn't dance."

"No, you had to go to Mexico City."

Gabriel remembered with perfect clarity the day he had gone to school dressed in his black suit and necktie and the teacher had said to him, "Gabriel, you are not going to dance. Lorenza Landero had to go out of town." And he had to sit by Doña Teresa, watching the others dance poorly, making mistakes on the steps that he had practiced until he knew them perfectly.

"No," said Lorenza, sighing deeply. "I didn't take a trip. Mamá didn't have enough money to buy me a dress and I couldn't tell people that. So I invented the story about the trip."

And after the confession she began to cry in her husband's arms as if she were once more a twelve-year-old girl.

"No, dear. Don't cry."

"I was in the house for a week with Mamá, crying and crying."

"My precious . . . Now . . . No, No."

The lie was still a lie, even though she had confessed it. It hurt her less but it was still there in her memory like an unchangeable fact. She had to recognize the stigma of belonging to a family of genteel poverty. She might have been happy if she had not been haunted by the thought of that greatness, that myth she must reconstruct in order to save herself. Reconstruct? Wouldn't it be simply a monstrous exaggeration of something ordinary and commonplace, elevated to another level? Oh no, not that. The Landeros . . . "The Landeros, my child, how shall I tell you? They were something very special. There are no longer any families like them." And Aunt Amelia lit a cigarette before continuing the explanation. "They were simply like nobody else. Wealthy, immensely wealthy. My grandmother, your great grandmother, drank a little too much one day and she began to throw gold coins out of the living room window. They say she was a show-off. Actually she was charming, delightful. Her husband, my grandfather, had something to do with the Reform Laws. The history books don't say anything about him but people who ought to know swear that it is true. Then came my father and by that time there wasn't so much money and you know how that tragedy began." "But my own father, what about my father?" "Your father! Well, Ernesto was a good man. Very good."

They say the same thing about Don Eusebio, she thought, coming back to reality. She saw Cristóbal pass in front of them at a gallop, riding one of the horses that belonged to the farm.

"That Cristóbal. Have you noticed? His eyes are green."

"No," Esther exclaimed. "They're black."

They saw him disappear on the other side of the pines.

"Come on, it's cold here. Let's go to my room." Suddenly she remembered. "And Eusebio?"

"He went to the stables with Gabriel."

"Oh!"

They went inside. In the hall Rita signaled to them that Doña Teresa was sleeping in a chair in the living room. They walked carefully on tiptoe to the winding staircase that led to Gabriel and Lorenza's quarters.

Esther looked at the living room and said, "Here the style undergoes a sudden change from rustic to baroque."

"Ah! What did you study?"

"In school, nothing. I read some things later on. I had plenty of time."

"I read, too," Lorenza said. "Detective stories and nothing but detective stories. I'll lend you some good ones."

"Oh, thanks, I'd like that. I love art books. I used to buy one whenever I went to Mexico City. I really don't know why I didn't bring them with me. Maybe I really didn't like them so much. I have a lot of them with reproductions: painting, sculpture . . . One of my favorite pastimes was looking at the pictures and imagining things. I used to read the text, too, but it wasn't very interesting. I like your things."

"And what did you expect?"

"Pardon?"

"Don't pay any attention to me. Sometimes I'm very unkind. Shall we ask Rita for some coffee, or would you like a drink?" Esther nodded that she would like a drink, and Lorenza went over to the chest to get the cognac. "You're right, this is a little baroque—maybe even very baroque. But that's because it's a kind of 'waiting room.' All these pieces are waiting for the day when they will be in their proper place. And someday," she said with an emphasis that seemed unnecessary, "they are going to be there."

After the third drink Lorenza felt depressed. Alejandro came in with an armful of logs and she asked him to light the fire. There really was no need of it, because the temperature was very agreeable, but within an hour night would fall and it would get cold. She noticed how the old man was putting the logs one on another as if he were weaving them and they caught fire immediately just as soon as he struck the match.

"They're nice and dry," Alejandro said.

"Yes, I see they are. And they're going to burn up quickly."

"Shall I bring some more?"

"Yes, please."

Alejandro disappeared.

"You are colder-natured than I am," Esther commented.

"I'm not really cold-natured, but fire makes me happy. It's so cheerful."

The two women looked at the flames as they became more and more intense.

Lorenza ran her fingers through her hair and asked, "What are you thinking about?"

"About Cuernavaca, about Mamá, about nothing, really . . . The fire is pretty."

A long silence followed and Esther was on the point of saying, "About Hugo," but the longer the silence lasted the more difficult it seemed for her to say the name of her husband and to express herself confidentially, in spite of the fact that the moment was propitious. Lorenza was the one who took advantage of it.

"It's not that I want to impress you, it's . . . that's the way I am. It sounds stupid, but it's the truth. When I was saying all that about lying, I wasn't talking just to be talking. I have my reasons."

She began to talk about the New Year celebration, about her dress. But she wasn't thinking about these things. She was really remembering another lie, another hidden embarrassment: the death of her father. Because he had too much to drink and too little to eat, because he lived in poverty, he had died of tuberculosis. When the doctor told them what sickness it was, he took them aside in a little room upstairs in that narrow house on Rojas street that was the last one the Landeros had owned. The doctor was a friend of the family and he didn't tell anyone. But he didn't have to tell anyone. Everybody knew it. His face, his color, his shoulders—everything indicated tuberculosis. And in spite of all that, when Don Ernesto died her mother had insisted on asking for a death certificate that called it a heart attack. The doctor gave it to her. And her mother went from friend to friend telling them all that her Ernesto had had heart trouble. Lorenza had also kept up the lie in school, even though it obliged her to repeat day after day the symptoms of the sickness that her father had never had. And she had done it on account of her mother's fear that the school doctor might examine her and find that she had caught tuberculosis and then the rich girls (there were still rich people in spite of the Landero's poverty) wouldn't have any more to do with her.

And that certainly would be inadmissible. Lorenza was better than any of them, better than all of them.

"Oh," she exclaimed, wishing to dismiss it, "it's all so horribly idiotic."

And yet she was not entirely convinced that it was. She still admired Aunt Amelia, she liked to think of her ancestors, and she liked to think of herself as "a Landero"—and she wanted *her* house.

Again she thought about deceiving Joaquina, about getting the money the very next day. But now she thought about it with much less certainty.

As if thinking about Joaquina had brought their thoughts together, Esther asked, "What are you saying about her?"

"About who?"

"About Joaquina."

"I haven't said a word about her all afternoon."

Esther felt upset. Then taking a chance, she asked the question.

"Lorenza, why don't Joaquina and Hugo like each other?"

"Because they're alike. Exactly alike."

"In what way?" Esther whispered. And then she dared to formulate the question that had refused to come out before. "What is Hugo like?"

Lorenza suddenly felt inspired by the question. Like a light turned on unexpectedly, she realized that she was in another world, thinking about other things, and that her sister-in-law had asked her something very serious, and that she ought to answer, she ought to say something immediately.

"He . . . he's . . . Oh! I don't know what you're talking about!"

She moved her hand as if she were trying to change something, to evade something. But what she wanted to evade, the reply to her own question, came decisively—Joaquina would never give her that money.

chapter 6

On the afternoons that Esther spent alone walking in and around the house, it seemed to her that there was something motionless. It was a something that managed to affect the nature of space—the landscape of pines veiled by mist, the crops of the communal farm—a something that in some strange way became a kind of token, a herald of eternity. "It's the static quality of the moment," Esther said to herself. "It's the absolute silence and the knowing that all this belongs to you."

It was this last impression that she came to understand and feel—she possessed something. The certainty of ownership lived within her. But where did it come from? The emissary wind from Cofre de Perote came down suddenly and frosted her cheeks, a clean wind with the smell of resin. Her feeling was born of a thousand foolish things, of memories, of intimate echoes, all coming from the same source: Hugo. The foolish words of love acquired specific and important meaning when her husband spoke them: "Who do you belong to?" "Who do I belong to?" Loving implies belonging absolutely to another person and at the same time belonging to oneself. And she had the same feeling with regard to the house. It belonged to her and yet it maintained its own integrity.

She was alone: the mistress of an afternoon that was silent and very much her own. The women were taking a siesta. Hugo and Gabriel had gone to the corral with Eusebio and the men— two cows were going to calve. Esther walked alone. She passed

by the chicken houses without paying attention and opened the
back gate. The noise of the arroyo was so weak that it sounded
like the tinkle of a toy. There was nobody washing clothes on
the bank. She looked at the fields, the clouds, the houses—distant,
scattered, very small—of the families who lived on the
communal farm. And she advanced slowly over her humid
kingdom—an emerald lawn as smooth as a carpet. She reached
the front steps and stood there several seconds. She had just
asked herself a question: "Do I love him as much as I used to?"
And she waited a minute to answer. "Yes, nothing has changed."
Then she continued her walk and climbed the steps. There were
flowers in her garden. She had spent a lot of time working in
it, and had planted lots of different things. Doña Teresa had invited
her friends from the Guild to have pastry one afternoon.
As soon as they found out about her garden project, they overwhelmed
her with slips and seedlings of all the varieties there
were in Las Vigas. "Your garden will be a beautiful miscellany,
a good example of the town's taste," Lorenza commented. "Remember
to plant what the most important ladies gave you in
prominent places, because if you don't, your relationships are
going to suffer a decline." Esther smiled when she remembered
the comment and pulled off some dry leaves. What looked best
was the honeysuckle that Cristóbal had set out under her instructions.
A thousand shoots were coming up. By August it
would be entirely green. "But it won't have flowers this year,
ma'am," Alejandro said. "Not until next year." Hugo enjoyed
seeing her work the land. "You should pay more attention to
your husband," he said laughing. "You're deserting me. There
are times when I'm not the center of your thoughts." And
Cristóbal, who heard the joke, picked up some stones hurriedly
and threw them in the wheelbarrow so he could carry them to
the other side of the house. The last thing she had planted was
a carnation that Hugo had brought her from town. "Plant it in
front of our window where I can see it when I get up."

Yes, she loved Hugo a great deal. But one thing had changed.
When she was first married she thought that her husband would
protect her from everything bad, that he would be her support,

her refuge. It wasn't that way. She was his support. She was the one who had to protect him.

"Esther dear . . ."

The voice, which she did not recognize, came from behind her. She turned rapidly and saw Luchita Ramírez, the president of the Guild, coming toward her with her awkward steps. Her long and narrow figure against the background of pines produced a strange effect—a stylized body whose presence served to make the lines of the pines different and human.

"Luchita," she said, getting up.

"A letter for you, dear. I'm bringing you a letter."

The Coviellas' correspondence always stayed at the post office until Don Anselmo, the postmaster, could send it by special messenger or by a friend.

Luchita Ramírez, whose age and looks would guarantee her virginity until her dying day, stopped in front of Esther and gave her a kiss.

"Lord help me, child, what a walk! I tell you I wouldn't have come if it hadn't been for you." She gave her the envelope. "I went by the post office and Don Anselmo told me that a letter had come for you, and he didn't have anyone to send it by, and since he says it's the first one you've gotten since you've been here, I offered to bring it to you. Imagine, honey . . . a month and a half without hearing anything from your family. And he says you've written about three letters. I tell you, Esther dear . . . this mail . . . Once it took a letter of mine twenty days to get here from Puebla. It's from your mamá, isn't it?"

"Yes, it's from Mamá."

"Read it. Don't bother about me. Anyway, I have to be going because I'm making a lot of calls on Guild members in connection with the Virgen del Carmen. How is Doña Teresa?"

"She's taking a siesta. Will you come in?"

"No, honey, I wish I could. Some other time. Give my regards to all of them. And you and Lorenza come to see us, whenever you can. We're always thinking about you."

She gave her another kiss and hurriedly went back toward town. Esther held the letter in her hands, watching Luchita disappear. She couldn't decide whether to open it or not, because she really didn't care what her mother had written. She tore it open.

She read between gusts of cold air. It was an almost statistical report of the number of tourists who had stayed at the hotel recently. Nothing about herself and not one question about the Coviella family. Nothing about how she had been, whether she was happy, what they were like, what the place was like, how they had treated her. Her mother, from the start of her relationship with Hans Meyer, had put aside anything that might imply intimacy. The letter had only one personal line, a complaint that had escaped under the guise of information: "Hans went to Acapulco again . . ."

"The funny thing is," she thought as she started up the hill without even realizing that she was climbing, "Hans Meyer no longer matters to me."

But there had been a time when he was important to her, and in an inevitable and definitive way. After she and her mother had worked alone for almost ten years, the business was going very well. In those days their income, although it was not very large, was consistent. The guests of the Posada de la Suerte were families of bureaucrats, traveling salesmen, and school teachers. It was a poor but decent clientele that gradually came to provide them a modest profit. Foreigners did not come to Señora Soto's inn except during Holy Week, when there were no other rooms available. On one such occasion Hans Meyer stayed there. Esther couldn't remember exactly when she had first been aware of his presence. She had seen him sitting at a table after dinner or after supper, smoking, looking over everything. Then she remembered seeing him talking with her mother. And one day, before anything happened, she looked at his milky skin, dry and stretched, and she noticed his prominent cheek bones, his excessively thin lips, and his eyes, eyes that could be pleasant. When her mother told her that they were going to be married, Esther couldn't recall just what day she had first guessed it. Was it the day she saw him examining the roof? Or was it the day she saw them holding hands? They were married in March of 1950 when she was almost seventeen. It was a "small wedding" for a hundred of Meyer's friends. She remembered it. She remembered it perfectly. There were Germans, Jews, and gringos, including some Negroes—an excessive number of affected and noisy men, and too many scandalously dressed women, all of them drinking vodka, tequila, or whisky without paying any attention to which it might be, and with little visible effect. The "foreign colony" (as Meyer called it) settled into the place from the time of the wedding. A week after the wedding the inn closed so that repairs might be made, or better said, new construction might be undertaken. They began by buying the neighboring houses and some vacant lots that were behind them and that could be bought very cheaply. Esther never knew exactly (the first obligation of which she was relieved was her duty as bookkeeper) how much capital her stepfather had put up. But she was sure that she and her mother had contributed more. The construction lasted more than eight months. When the grand opening was celebrated—with advertisements in the daily papers of Mexico City—the Meyers were up to their necks in debt. Esther and her mother had stopped being "the Sotos." Now the world recognized her mother as part of "the Meyers," and that naturally excluded Esther. She lived in one of the rooms on the second floor—"We have so many customers, dear, we don't have enough space"— while her mother and Hans lived in the first bungalow, one of a row of twenty that had been built on the recently purchased land. At the back of the property, in the center, they built an enormous swimming pool. All the innovations were accompanied by the continually weakening warnings of Esther. "But Mamá, think of the cost. It's a very expensive thing. Where are we going to get the money for a luxury hotel? They will end up suing us for everything that we've earned with ten years' work. Try to see, Mamá, try to see. Don't live in the clouds." But Doña Esther did live in the clouds and they didn't get sued either. After a year and a half the Nueva Posada de la Suerte was receiving the "most exclusive" clientele of Cuernavaca. If an ambassador, a movie star, a great politician, or a millionaire visited the city, he stopped there. The bank account of Señora Meyer changed from pesos to dollars, and her daughter stopped having anything to do with it. They tried to pay her off in order to keep her happy: "Genuine American clothing, dear. Who would have dreamed of that?"

And they told her (Hans was the one who did the telling), "From now on you will not have to work at all. We want you to enjoy yourself."

"Not to work, they wanted me to enjoy myself," she said to herself, leaning her hand against a pine. She couldn't weep about that anymore. She crushed the letter and put it in one of her skirt pockets. No, it doesn't matter to me any more, she thought, shaking her head. She looked at the Coviella's house. "It's mine," she said. "I love it—and it's mine." She smiled.

"I talk like Hugo. I feel like Hugo." She said it in a very low voice, and caressed the trunk of the pine tree as tenderly as she caressed her husband's cheek and hair, feeling herself the owner.

In Cuernavaca Esther used to take walks through the hotel garden after dinner. The paths were bordered by intensely colored bougainvillaeas and acacias. It was an endless contest between color and heat, and during the sweaty hours of siesta time she would go and find a seat on one of the wicker chairs close to the swimming pool. The excessive light—the blinding sparks on the water—made her close her eyes. Her eyelids fell heavily and she entered a dark red world where her monologues found the words of the inexpressible and showed the nothingness of her existence. Often she tried to reconstruct the image of her first home. It was a large house in Colonia Juárez, built during the time of Porfirio Díaz. Her parents had lived in the back part of it because her mother had insisted that it was too spacious for just the three of them, and besides, they could rent the front part. The house had a pretty garden in front where she could not play because she was not supposed to bother the tenants. She had forgotten how the house was built, retaining only fragments of memory: a corner in the laundry room, a dark hallway with a wardrobe against the wall . . . a scene: her father

cutting paper dolls for her. Nothing more. The scream of a
tourist snatched her out of the memory. She opened her eyes
and again saw the pool, the trees, the vines. She felt like a
woman who waits in a park for someone who will never come,
and still does not feel deceived, because she has always known
he wouldn't come, and nevertheless will stay there just in case
he might appear. Often her eyes would focus on a masculine
body and stay there—windows open to excitement. An impulse
would prompt her to move, to go close to the water. Several
times she had tried to love. Two engagements with no consequences, both characterized by boredom. Two errors because
she paid attention to her mother's counsel: "It's time for you . . ."

The notes from Lorenza's piano reached Esther there at the
edge of the woods. She wanted to live there all her life, to be
happy with Hugo, to make him happy. They had told her that
winter here was long, difficult. She looked forward to the coming of the cold weather that would make them stay inside the
house with the doors and windows closed. Doña Teresa wanted
to teach her to knit. Of course, she would knit infant's clothing.
Maybe. Why not? By that time . . . We will have a child, my
child, Hugo's child.

"Psst."

Surprised, she looked to see who was calling her. She saw the
pigsties and Alejandro's house. No one was there. Her heart
began to beat rapidly and she thought of something that frightened her—something she had never thought of before. She kept
on walking slowly in order not to deceive herself with her own
steps. For several seconds she had had the disagreeable certainty that it was Cristóbal who had called her, the certainty
also of an imminent nearby danger.

"Psst, psst."

This time it was impossible to think it was imagination. There
was someone behind Alejandro's door. But how could anyone
have the nerve? How could anyone dare? Slowly the door
opened. She could scream, or she could run. No, she would take
care of him. She was not going to permit such a lack of respect.

First she felt herself staring at his unpleasant grin, then terror overcame her. The man, in the shadow, staggered. It was Hugo.

"Come in," he ordered.

Later on Esther remembered that her relief had been so great that she had not even reproached him.

"What time did you get back?"

But Hugo didn't answer. Her fear seemed to amuse him.

"Come have a drink with the boss." He led her to the bar, where he had just opened a bottle of rum. "Here, señora, it's an honor to drink with me. The men feel honored that I, the boss, drink with them. So! You charm me when you smile, when you're happy. A moment ago your face looked like a frightened donkey's. I want you to be happy, young, my unconditional companion, not my judge, not even half my judge. I don't want criticism or arguments. I don't want you and me to quarrel ever for anything. Drink because it's time to celebrate and because today is my afternoon off. Just like the maids I gave myself a chance to rest. I gave myself a vacation."

"The boss," said Esther tenderly.

Hugo was going to light a cigarette. He put the match, already burning, close to his wife's chin. The flame illuminated her skin and her eyes.

"The world's most beautiful woman," he said and lit the cigarette. Esther felt very sure of herself. She had not made a mistake when she married him.

"I'm so stupid, such a fool. You'll have to pardon me."

"Why didn't you go to the corral?"

"Because Joaquina told me to."

He looked at her. Was she perhaps his enemy? He served himself another shot and drank it in one swallow.

"I didn't go because I've had enough. Because I'm not going to spend every day of my life doing what she orders me to do. I work like a dog. And my father worked for her for twenty-five years. Isn't that enough? Hasn't that earned anything? What she has is also ours. A good part of hers is mine. Mine!"

"Don't shout," Esther said. She came over to him, caressed

him, and leaned against his chest. "Nobody is arguing with you about anything. She hasn't even reprimanded you."

"Don't defend her."

"I am not defending her. It's just that . . ."

"Shut up."

He pushed her away brusquely and she hit the bar, causing the bottle of rum to fall on the floor.

"I'll buy another one," he shouted immediately. "I'm not going to stop drinking. I'll buy another one. Wait! I have some more right here. I'd forgotten." He ran to Alejandro's room and came back opening the new bottle, calm and smiling. Then he saw that his wife was crying. "But you . . . but I . . . I don't want you to cry. Forgive me. Okay?"

chapter 7

Doña Teresa decided to stay in the car. The stable had a disagreeable smell and she knew the pasture by heart. She could perfectly well say a rosary while they were taking a walk. Eusebio was running and shouting ahead of his parents.

"That child," Doña Teresa exclaimed, sticking her head out the window. "You watch him! Don't let him get too close to the animals!"

Lorenza made a slight movement of her shoulders without taking the trouble to answer and then started running in the opposite direction. She was tired of her mother-in-law. The old lady had spent all morning talking about the church, God, the devil, confession, absolution, and the Guild. She had had enough. That's why she had proposed the walk through the pasture, to get away from her absurd role of complaisant listener on those days when Doña Teresa talked interminably about religion. "She used not to be that way," Gabriel had often said. "It's an obsession that started with Papá's death." Lorenza thought to herself that it was more than an obsession. She ran on toward a little hill where there were some sickly oak trees. It was madness; she was absolutely mad.

"Go on, follow Mamá," Gabriel ordered.

Eusebio saw his mother's silhouette moving in the distance. "I'm coming too. Run!"

But the child did not move. His enormous eyes, so vulnerable and unreservedly tender, were fixed on the hypodermic needle.

He followed Alejandro's movements as if he were in a trance and suffered a slight shock when he saw the cow tremble and suddenly jerk.

"Why are they doing that? What are they putting in her?"

"Calcium, so she won't get sick. Let's go." Gabriel took him by the hand and led him away.

It was a beautiful August afternoon, the apple-scented wind filled the atmosphere with something sweet and clean. A golden light flooded the grassland, the countryside was an incorruptible simplicity. Gabriel was suddenly filled with happiness. Living was sometimes an infinite revelation of fullness capable of sweeping away the continuous and innumerable little worries and conflicts that make life spend itself in a prison of boredom and antagonism—everything within very narrow limits that require the daily repetition of the commonplace in a slow game of stupidities. The afternoon was using the wind to sing its splendor. A wind that blew Eusebio's chestnut hair. Gabriel thought of himself when he was a boy. An older boy. A march— his hair also blown by the wind—the childish voices of his schoolmates:

> Laborers, let us march to our fields
> to sow there the healthy seed of progress;
> let us march together always straight and strong,
> working for the peace of our nation.
> Let brother no longer spill the blood of brother . . .

"Do you remember?" he asked, interrupting his song and walking close to Lorenza.

"Yes, but it's the first time I've heard it for years."

The three of them sat down on the grass. Lorenza kept on humming the march.

"Most often calves are born in the summertime, and then they inject the cows with calcium in order to avoid 'milk fever.' This one will have a calf in a week at the latest," Hugo said, pointing out a beautiful brown specimen who was looking at them with her sad eyes. "You like her? She's a gem."

"Yes," Esther answered just to please him. What she really liked was the enthusiasm that her husband showed when he spoke of each animal. She smoothed her hair and in the distance saw Gabriel and Lorenza sitting on the grass. She could hear a murmur. Are they singing? The wind mussed her hair again and she decided not to pay any attention to it. She had already asked: How many liters do they give? How much do they cost? How many are there? Then she tried to think of another question and said: "Do they get sick often?"

"Well, here in this climate, not very much. When they do, it's generally some respiratory difficulty that we cure with antibiotics. Since it's too cool here for ticks, we don't have to worry about the more serious illnesses. That one had a calf that we sold day before yesterday. Now she's giving more than twenty liters a day. And what milk! Come look at the little calves."

He took her by the hand. Esther went with him without really being interested. It was her first visit and she ought to see everything. Hugo, on the other hand, was having a wonderful time. He was enjoying showing his wife where he spent the hours when he was not by her side, and he was glad to have her understand the importance of his work and to see how well he knew the animals (much better than Gabriel, in spite of the fact that he has been here longer than I have). Hugo also knew that at that very moment Joaquina was looking at them from Liborio's house and he was absolutely sure that it pleased his aunt to see him moving about down there explaining it all enthusiastically. And so she (Joaquina) would pardon his little sprees as easily as he justified them to himself. One more drink. Sometimes twenty more. But I work. I am well aware of this and she knows that nobody takes advantage of me or robs me of a cent. She loves me. I know she loves me a great deal. Papá told me that when I was born, she wanted me to be her own. Her son. He was such an easy-going type, he might have given me to her. What a deal for me. Now I would be the owner of all of this. Absolutely the owner of the whole business. The old girl really isn't bad. The bad part is that sometimes she behaves like a bitch toward me. She knows how to behave properly toward everybody else. She never fusses with Gabriel the way she fusses with me. But I'm sure she would give her life for me before she would for him. Well, I don't want her to kill herself. It's all right with me just for her to die.

"What are you laughing at?" Esther asked.

"Nothing."

Liborio had been working for Doña Joaquina Coviella for thirteen years, thirteen years of relative harmony and general agreement; but in spite of that, he still felt that one of his great problems in life was a visit from Joaquina to the stable. Today —as if she were proof of his dread—there she was in front of him holding some wet boxes in her large strong hands, boxes of "concentrated balanced feed."

"Thirteen! Thirteen!" she cried, pointing to the boxes she held in her hands and also the ones she had thrown aside.

"The trouble is, these guys don't know how to take care of things. They're nothing but Indian bums."

"But you have been working for me for thirteen years. They are not the ones I hold responsible. You are. What on earth are you thinking about? I permit you to live here with your wife, your children, your aunts and uncles, your cousins, and your friends. And all of you drink my milk. Well, I accept it and it doesn't matter to me. I have too much anyway. Very well. But take care of what is mine. Take care of it! And I beg you, Liborio—this is the last time that I am going to say it—I beg you not to blame anybody else. If something bad happens here the only one to blame is yourself. And besides, you're as Indian as they are and don't pretend you're not."

Joaquina threw down the boxes she was holding. Her displeasure vanished as soon as she had expressed it in shouting and gesticulating. I have told this idiot so many times that it is the last time I am going to beg him to do anything. She shrugged her shoulders and walked toward the door. And I have never really begged him. I don't know why I tell him that it's the last time I am going to beg him. Maybe because he makes me believe it. He is a good man, and now he is old, and not one of his sons is worth half as much as he is. I am going to miss him when he dies. She looked at the hill where the oak trees were. Eusebio was playing with his parents. "Why don't I despise Lorenza?" she asked herself. "Why? It's because she is not a fool. That's the only reason. Actually her name is worth less in money than my own is. No, they're not going to catch me up on my past. In this country—the idiots—a person's background is based on color. Color is more important. I am whiter than she is, a lot whiter." And in spite of that she would never be able to free herself from Lorenza's superiority. She knew it perfectly well. She bit her lips, remembering her father with fury. Her father, the master of a vocabulary of bad words that he used for saying dirty and uncalled-for things. Why doesn't my hate stop? Why doesn't it?

She went outside into the light and the wind kissed her cheeks with a smack. She saw Esther and Hugo go into the stables and heard his voice. Suddenly she grew tender. In the middle of that luminous and inopportune afternoon she wanted to cry. She didn't want to be there. She longed for the intimacy of a room, the complicity of walls, the narrowness of a small and hermetic place, where she could explain (to someone who really cared) that she was not bad, that she was lonely, that she needed the absolute surrender of Hugo, his absolute love. Nothing abnormal. She didn't mean an abnormal relationship. She loved him as only Teresa could love him, or even more. As if she were a better mother. And she would never, never, never tell him so.

She rubbed her eyes as if the light had blinded her. Looking over to where Doña Teresa sat in the automobile she saw three of the men passing by and greeting her.

Esther saw them coming. Her subconscious inclination to draw back, to hide, made her blush. Why? She took a few steps forward in their direction so no one could possibly think that she was trying to hide. "It is illogical," she said to herself, "it is illogical that I should try not to see him. He hasn't done anything against me. He is absolutely nothing but a field worker like all the rest."

"Good afternoon, señora." The three men spoke together.

"Good afternoon," she said with the hint of a smile.

Cristóbal, Lucio, and Francisco kept on toward Liborio's house, where some children came out to meet them. Esther breathed a sigh of relief. On the basis of the fright that Hugo had caused her she began to analyze her feeling. Why had she thought—before anything else—that it was Cristóbal? And that night, beside her sleeping husband, she recalled a series of smiles, blushes, little attentions and kindnesses that Cristóbal had shown toward her. Something that, at the moment it happened, could be reasonably explained (although as a matter of fact she didn't think about explanations) as the reflection of simple affection toward her husband. And in her case it could be extended and even exaggerated into an awkward (they are field hands) desire to be unquestionably at her service. That is all. What bothered her was that her later reaction was the reserved position of an observer. But, an observer of what? She asked herself the question in the kitchen when she was serving coffee. Of him? Of myself? The problem was unreasonably complicated and pointless. Because I love Hugo, because I want only my husband. Because I am satisfied with him.

The test, favorable for her, had ended. The men (Cristóbal) were playing with Liborio's dogs and grandchildren. The air brought a certain calm with it and instantly it seemed to her that the whole business had been a tempest in a teapot. Why must we be so complicated? Why be so subtle about little things? Why this bitterness toward each other? As always, she blamed everything on Hans Meyer. He had taught her to be suspicious of everything and everybody. And especially of him.

"What?" she said, answering the tap on her shoulder rather than the voice that had called her.

"My aunt is talking to us."

It had been a long time since Gabriel had thought about his years in elementary school, but Lorenza kept humming "The Ballad of the Field Hand," and it brought that past time to mind. A strange thing had happened. For two years they sang:

Many of our brothers gave their lives
in the struggle for justice and love.
May God keep them in heaven above.

Then one morning the principal—dark, round, shining—came
into the auditorium and summoned the teachers, interrupting
the song. Gabriel saw them and heard them arguing, raising
their voices, gesticulating. Finally the singing hour was suspended and they all went out for recess until the problem was
resolved. An hour of games and races. Back in the classroom,
the teacher began by saying: "Write in your notebooks 'The
Ballad of the Field Hand.' He dictated it aloud in spite of the
fact that they all knew it by heart. And then he ordered the
change: "In place of 'May God keep them in heaven above,' you
are to sing 'And set us a worthy example.' "

He didn't give any explanation of the change and that set up
a series of predictable misunderstandings—on the part of pupils
and teachers—that ended up by causing the cancellation of the
singing classes.

Gabriel smiled: Who do you suppose was fired for the error?
Because undoubtedly there was someone to blame, or an imbecile who had not realized that they, "the ones who will grow
up in a socialist era," did not believe in God.

Their education (his and Lorenza's) had been "experimental," as he told his wife while they sat watching Eusebio run
around, sweaty and indefatigable.

"And we were caught halfway through the 'experiment,' "
she answered. "We never found out the results. Or do you
know them?"

"Well, at least there's one thing certain: I'll never let Eusebio
be taught by nuns. He will go to public school, just as we did."

"I'm not against it," Lorenza answered. "Eusebio is a boy."

"I don't think sex has anything to do with it."

"I think it does. A girl needs to be a little presumptuous. She
must be something superior and different from the majority of
girls."

"The ones who will grow up in a socialist era." Gabriel re-

membered his first day in elementary school—the sixth of January, 1934. After calling the roll and casting several inquisitorial and awe-inspiring looks at them, the teacher asked, "Who got presents from the Three Wise Men?" The majority of the children raised their hands. Only the poorest ones looked at the floor, abject and miserable. Then the teacher began to explain to them that their fathers were liars, fakes, dirty . . . That she— all of the teachers—were going to save them from the pernicious influence of their families. The Wise Men do not exist! God does not exist! Your parents are liars, they are deceiving you. But you, you have the privilege of beginning in a new era. You are the ones who will grow up in a socialist era. Truth and justice will reign. My children (beseechingly), never believe in your parents. But during recess one child affirmed that *he* had *seen* the Three Wise Men. And if the teacher said they didn't exist, it was because she was bad and ugly, and for that reason nobody should believe anything she said.

"It's not a question of being presumptuous," Gabriel said, "but of learning. He also has to learn to doubt. I prefer 'experiments,' unilateral ways, in spite of the fact that now I want to be solid and capitalistic and that's all I think about. But I want my son to have problems."

"Don't worry, he will have them."

O Lamb of God, who takest away the sins of the world: forgive us, O Lord. O Lamb of God, who takest away the sins of the world: hear us, O Lord. O Lamb of God, who takest away the sins of the world: have mercy on us.

Doña Teresa's arthritic fingers put her rosary away in her purse. She crossed herself several times and then smoothed her skirt. Father Miguel had told her a thousand times that she mustn't weep any more over the death of Eusebio. But she couldn't help it, she was going to cry. She blinked several times. The landscape: light was on the grass and on the road, and it appeared and disappeared, but she could not weep. Astonished, she tried it again. It's impossible. It can't be. A small and malignant laugh rose to her lips. She wanted not to laugh, she tried to hold it back by clenching her teeth. But an absurd, confused sound came from her mouth and it made her burst out laughing harder and harder, until the excess brought tears to her eyes and she wept abundantly. There he was with his eyes already closed. I couldn't see them. There was not a sign of a blow on his face, not even the slightest scratch. It seems that he closed his eyes when he saw that he was going to crash, and the steering column pierced his chest. But his eyes! His eyes! He never opened them again. They were so blue, so beautiful! Neither of his sons inherited that color—nor his grandson. That horrible afternoon. I will always remember that afternoon when I thought I would never go to the city again.

chapter 8

The automobile turned into a narrow road bordered by slender pear trees that from a distance looked like cypresses. Their intensely green, clean leaves hid the pears—stains of gold, guessed more than seen, as the car passed rapidly. The road led them to an enormous apple orchard and Esther was astonished at the quantity of fruit. The branches were hanging to the ground, weighed down by their own red burden.

"I want one," Eusebio shouted.

"Wait a minute," she asked him.

Hugo stopped the car and got out with them. Eusebio ran to the nearest apple tree. The sun was lighting his eyes, and Esther smiled. Suddenly his joy turned into crystal laughter. Spontaneous and unmotivated, it infected his two companions, and the three of them laughed happily for no reason at all. The fear with which Esther had accepted the ride turned into joy. Hugo had taken her forcibly from the kitchen, against her will and her saying, "No, Hugo, dinner isn't finished." Her protests were accompanied by the laughter of Rita, who always enjoyed these scenes that changed her routine and made her a participant in the relationships of the Coviella family.

They were three refugees, hungry for laughter and merriment, and ready to find it anywhere. For no reason at all they took each other by the hand—Eusebio in the middle—and started a crazy race among the apple trees. The trunks of the trees seemed to travel at their sides, rapid, close. Shapes were joined to other shapes by the speed of their flight, which amidst their laughter obliged them to watch their step, to be careful of a stone, to jump over a hole here and there, then on again. Eusebio was flying, the apple held in his teeth, laughter engraved on his features, his eyes closed by the force of the wind, his feet barely touching the grass from time to time. A nervous laugh (the sensation of falling) made his apple drop to the ground and end up who knows where, without his having time even to notice.

A wire fence brought the game to an end. Fatigue replaced laughter on their sun-reddened faces. Breathing rapidly, Esther saw another farm on the other side of the fence, other apple trees loaded with fruit, other field hands with wooden packing crates. And she loved feeling the wind cool her cheeks. Suddenly she heard a crawling, dragging noise that broke the charm and innocence of the moment.

"Are there snakes here?" she asked, suddenly frightened, feeling that she didn't belong there.

"Certainly. There are apples. Remember the Bible."

"No, Hugo. Don't laugh. Oh!"

The two of them looked at the grass that waved almost noiselessly—waves that were not caused by the wind. It moved first slowly and then fast, then slow again, hesitating.

"It's a squirrel!" Hugo exclaimed. "Look at it!"

When the squirrel saw them, it disappeared at top speed, uselessly followed by Eusebio.

They went back to the car and continued their ride across other farms. The houses of the field hands were scattered along the road and as they passed, the children came out to see them, shouting "Hi, hi." The car went up a small hill and between two oak trees, then entered a wood of ferns and pines on whose trunks dwelt strange lichens with leaves that looked like the petals of red flowers.

"Look down to your right," Hugo said, stopping the car. "That's El Bordo."

They were on the peak, at the edge of an abyss. For Esther the first impression was unreal. She felt that she was witnessing something that could not be expressed or even retained in words, and that this scene—the sudden and deep break in the earth, those small, scarcely perceptible houses on the other side (houses like points or stains on grass in every shade of green and accented by the snow)—was nothing but the reflection of some illusion. It was a bedazzling, irrational panorama without definite limits, because the fog made a kind of mirage of what had been precise and exact only a moment earlier. Color, distance, and depth all moved to the rhythm of the mist. Something was happening there that seemed not to happen within time.

Silently they got out of the car. Esther walked and felt as if she were walking in some kingdom foreign to man. She looked at the strips of snow close against the opposite side, and to her they appeared to be symbols of the amorphous, of the uncomprehended, of the vague, the divine, the beautiful. Something that acknowledged and explained the presence and significance of her and of Hugo in this world. Something capable of transcending all logic.

"This is my retreat," Hugo said. "You will very rarely see it this way. Fog covers it nearly the whole year long."

"His retreat," she repeated to herself, walking over the moss-draped rocks. "This is where he comes to hide from everyone, from himself if necessary." There was something in the atmosphere, in its quietness, that could erase hatred, limitations, misery. Vaguely she felt that there was something there that in a primordial fashion, and as a salvation, offered the possibility and acceptance of religious mystery. She felt capable of believing again all that she had forgotten, either by denying it or repressing it . . . And I can reconstruct all the world's myths.

"The town you see there in front, those houses, is called Tatatila. One day I'll go there on foot. I'll get up early with one of the men . . ."

"A myth," interrupted Esther. "A myth for me, for us. Yes, it's truly ours. You should have brought me here before. This snow . . . this place . . . this child."

Hugo looked at Eusebio, who was playing with a branch,

brandishing it like a sword, and then at his wife. Esther was moving about very slowly, bedazzled, phantasmal, translated.

"A child. A child of yours, Esther. I want a child of our own."

"For the time being I am not interested in buying anything. Yes . . . yes." Joaquina nervously rolled and unrolled the telephone cord with her index finger. "Your last recommendation turned out to be a complete failure. They are going to widen the street and take ten yards from the front. No . . . Yes . . . All right, I'll expect you in the morning."

She hung up the telephone disgustedly. Her steps echoed loudly in the halls, then she went into the living room and found Lorenza and Gabriel in front of the recently lighted fireplace. The clock was at half past one.

"I don't think it's cold!" she said sarcastically.

"I am cold," Lorenza answered, standing erect.

"Why must you always quarrel?" Gabriel asked. "Can't we live in peace and do what we want to do?"

"That's what you always do. I don't see why you have to complain. If you paid attention to me . . . a little less wood and a little less cognac, we would have more money."

"You're right. We'd have a lot more. We could also learn not to eat."

"A drink will do you good, Joaquina. It will calm your nerves," Lorenza said, serving her.

"Give me one too, child," said Doña Teresa, who was praying as she sat in the rocking chair close to the window. "I don't know what they could be doing. I'm so worried. I've already prayed three rosaries for them. Do you think they are all right?"

"Don't worry. He's probably in town getting drunk," Joaquina commented.

"With the child and Esther? Impossible. They went for a ride."

"During working hours."

"There was nothing to do and you know it perfectly well," Gabriel interrupted.

"Everybody agrees with everybody else just to be against me."

"I don't, Joaquina. I think you are right and I'm on your side."

"Yes, you and your rosaries. Some help!"

Gabriel served himself another drink, lit a cigarette, and lay down on the sofa where he could watch the fire. He heard his mother's voice: "I always remember Eusebio, who went away just the way they did, and they brought him back to me dead." That is what she remembered. What she had forgotten was that Don Eusebio had drunk much more than he should have that day. Gabriel thought about his brother. He couldn't possibly be getting drunk. It displeased him that Aunt Joaquina was always distrustful and recriminatory toward Hugo. He had to admit there was plenty of reason for her attitude. Time after time, for years now, he (Gabriel) had waited on that same sofa for his brother to come back, finally going out to look for him. Almost always with the certainty, in those last moments, that this time something had indeed happened . . . And the hours of waiting always created this atmosphere of discontent and tension that gradually dominated them so that they began to argue with each other. Suddenly the waiting period would turn into an opportunity to verbalize insults and accusations. It had been that way since his childhood, and he was twenty-five years old before he discovered that the quarrels had a healthy effect and that, apart from any other advantages, they served to smooth over Hugo's return, so he was accepted again without reproach. And that always put off the tremendous final scene, full of wrath and hate. Gabriel himself, during one of these times of waiting, had come to hate his brother for dragging them to an extreme of irritability that threatened to last forever and make their lives definitively impossible. But when Hugo was there with him again, hate disappeared quietly and he was happy to have him at home, protected. Because Hugo needed his love, his help . . . Not so much now, now he had Esther by his side and the improvement was obvious—the stability he had achieved. Suddenly he was surprised by the clarity with which he heard the crackling of the logs. He looked at his family. Everyone was silent. He didn't like it. He would rather have— maybe because he was used to it—the explosions, the daily repetition of disagreement and disapproval.

"What's happening to you? Have another cognac."

"If they haven't gotten here by two o'clock, we will have dinner," Joaquina said, looking at her watch.

Lorenza served the drinks.

"There, there's the car," Doña Teresa exclaimed.

No one got up. The first one in the living room was Eusebio, then Esther.

"We had a marvelous ride and are as tired as we can be."

"We are tired too," said Joaquina, "tired of waiting for you. You left dinner half prepared. Which of your servants did you order to finish it for you?"

Esther's happiness disappeared. Lorenza saw her become pale.

"I finished it," Lorenza said. And then she lied, "She asked me to do it."

"Well, Hugo didn't let me . . . He made me go . . . I told him that . . ."

"The men don't give orders here. We women do."

"I give orders to my wife," said Hugo in the doorway.

"Magnificent. Can you tell me who lent you the car?"

"I told him when they were married that he could use it whenever he wished," Gabriel said.

"We saw a squirrel in the country," Eusebio shouted suddenly.

"Be quiet!" Joaquina ordered. "When grown-ups are talking . . ."

Hugo burst out laughing.

"You see her?" he asked, speaking to Esther. Then to his aunt: "Just a few minutes ago she told me I was exaggerating when I said something about your bad disposition." He continued laughing while he served himself some cognac. "And I bet her that today you would explode. You've helped me win twenty pesos. And you still haven't seen her at her worst. When she reaches her peak, she insults me and strikes me dead with her eyes. I feel like wringing her neck and she'd like to draw and quarter me."

"Cynic! Fool!"

"Dear God in heaven! Please don't start it, don't start it."

Hugo kept on laughing. Cognac ran down his chin. He wiped it off and filled his glass again.

"Get drunk! That's all we need!" Joaquina shouted. Suddenly she looked at him carefully. "No, now I see. You're drunk already." She looked at Esther. "Where was he drinking?"

"They gave us a drink at Lucha Ramírez' house. We went by to visit her. He isn't drunk. He had one drink of anisette, just as I did."

"Don't explain anything to her," Gabriel shouted.

"Mamá, can we go to see the squirrel this afternoon?"

"I'm the one who shouts around here."

"We can all shout, you're not the only one who has the privilege."

"Lorenza, keep quiet!"

"Don't shout at me!"

"Tell me, darling, what was the squirrel like?"

"Money, money. Money is privilege."

"Money, crap."

"Hugo, you said, you told me . . . remember."

"I expected as much, that's the only reply you're capable of."

"The little squirrel. Let the child talk. For God's sake, let the child talk. Tell me, son, what was the squirrel like?"

"I am not talking to you!" She turned rapidly toward Hugo. "Explain yourself. Why did you do it? Who lent you the car?"

"Nobody."

"Oh, so you took it just because you wanted to, just because it was your pleasure. Is it yours?"

"Gabriel, make them stop!"

"My God, my God. Why don't we understand you? Why must we fight every day? Hail Mary, Mother of God."

"Mamá, I'm hungry."

"Come here, Eusebio, I'll talk to you. Your grandmother . . ."

"Wait, wait."

"It was not just a whim. I think I deserve it."

"Hugo, be quiet!"

"Leave him alone. Let him keep on. Let's see, so you deserve it? Why? When did you pay for it?"

"Doña Joaquina, it's my fault. I should have refused, but . . ."

"Don't offer her explanations," Lorenza shouted.

Now Joaquina was laughing.

"No, certainly not. Why? You are free, you are rich."

"Don't shout, Joaquina. I am on your side. They will soon calm down. Blessed Mother of God, calm them. Calm them!"

"Cut out that stuff about calming them. There are no madmen here. Everyone is sane."

"Don't cry, my son. You have frightened him."

"Doña Joaquina, I . . ."

"No, not you. You don't have to surrender! Be quiet! She hates me. Don't you see? You'd like to see me dead, wouldn't you?"

"Hugo! Calm down! Let's eat. Come on, Aunt Joaquina, come on."

"Ah, yes, the good brother, the peacemaker . . . Let them insult you, deny you what you deserve . . . Shit! And nobody's going to tell me not to have another drink."

"Don't have one!"

"I accept that. No more drinks. I'll have the whole bottle."

"Hugo, my darling."

"Hugo, my son, for God's sake."

"You animal!"

"Hugo!"

"You idiot, you'll ruin yourself!"

But what was left in the bottle—more than half—went down rapidly. Gabriel snatched it away from him when it was already empty. Hugo began to laugh joylessly without seeing anyone.

"Another bottle, Aunt Joaquina, another bottle. I've paid for them."

"You imbecile! You beast! We've had enough of your farce and enough of your lack of respect. This is my house. I am the boss here, and the car and the cognac are mine too."

"Screw you! They are as much mine as they are yours."

Joaquina slapped him rapidly—two, five times—to the astonishment of everyone. Hugo's eyes and cheeks reddened suddenly, his veins swelled. Everyone could see his anger clearly during the movement when he lifted his arm to strike her—a movement that was never completed. His arm fell heavily and then, driven by rage, he left the room.

"Hugo! Don't go!" Doña Teresa and Esther shouted at the same time.

Nobody tried to stop him. The automobile engine sounded immediately. Gabriel clutched his glass desperately.

"He ought not to go," Esther whispered between sobs. "He ought not to. He will hurt himself."

Lorenza ran to the window. She saw him disappear. Before her eyes there was only the heavy fog. She turned around, furious, and exclaimed, "If anything happens, Joaquina, you are . . ." But she did not finish.

Her words died when she saw the distorted face, the desperate tears of their aunt.

chapter 9

Saturnino Linares, at fifty-six years, was a notary, a member of the Company of Jesus, and a prominent associate in the ownership of the city's two casinos. He allowed Rita, who hadn't the slightest idea how important he was, to lead him to Joaquina's office.

"You look even sicker than usual," Joaquina said to him by way of greeting.

"And you are just as humorous as always," he answered, sitting down before receiving the invitation that never would come anyway. "My wife sends her greetings."

"Is she still alive?"

Saturnino recognized the joke with a little laugh.

"Yes, and if she had any idea what a beautiful garden you have here she would have come to give you some chrysanthemum cuttings. Something different. She bought them in Mexico City last year, from those Japanese florists."

"What do you want, Saturnino? Why have you come?"

The attorney Saturnino Linares laughed another little laugh, very appropriate to his white skin and his almost green eyes. Then a light blush came to his cheeks, anticipating the rosy glow they would have by late afternoon.

"Well, first of all, here's a letter. I went to the Spanish Casino for an aperitif two days ago and the manager told me that he had received a letter for you . . . from Puebla . . . from Spanish Charities."

He handed her the letter and Joaquina tossed it on the desk without taking the trouble to open it. Then she stared at him again and Saturnino continued:

"In the second place, and more important for both of us, a sale. That is, a purchase for you . . . a bargain." He paused in order to give his piece of news the proper importance. "The Landero house."

"The Landero house," Joaquina repeated.

Saturnino Linares laughed again, approvingly.

"It is your opportunity, Joaquina."

The attorney observed his client Joaquina Coviella, "Widow of Larragoitia," as it said on the oldest dossier that he had inherited from his predecessor, Don Anselmo Borrego. He was pleased with himself for having given his sentence an appropriate dual emphasis: without saying anything indelicate, he had alluded to the need for family background that Joaquina had suffered for twenty years, and he had also referred to the advantage of a good business deal.

"My opportunity," she repeated absent-mindedly, without understanding.

"Of course. You have been wanting that house for twenty years."

Joaquina looked at him and was disgusted, just as she always was, when she noticed his mannerisms, his caricature of an English gentleman.

"You are mistaken, sir," she said slowly. "I have not spent twenty years wanting that house. I wanted it twenty years ago. But I don't want it now."

"Oh, Joaquina! We know each other. Fortunately I've known you for so long I am not offended. If you should offend me I would leave here immediately and offer this opportunity to someone else, because you know as well as I do that any family in Jalapa would like to buy the Landero house."

"If that were the case, you wouldn't be here."

"Joaquina, your intelligence and your caustic wit have always intrigued me. If you had wanted to be a society lady you would have gone far with your face, your bearing, your . . ."

"How much are they asking for it?"

". . . talent. For you . . . for you, two hundred thousand pesos.
That price is only for you, and I am not lying. It's a whim of the
owner. He is a romantic person, in love with the property, truly
in love with it, and he would like to sell it to you because you
are rich and related to Lorenza Landero."

"My business deals are entirely separate from my family ties."

"I knew it. Bravo! It is what I told him you would say. I ad-
mire you, Joaquina, and that's why I came here to propose it
to you. Buy it! It is worth much more. That corner is absolutely
the best in Jalapa and I swear to you that there will be no
changes. You are protected. It is in the same block as the best
colonial corner in the city—that's the way they advertise it in
the tourist propaganda, 'the best colonial corner in the city.'
They are architectural jewels. Nobody would ever think of
widening that street. It combines local color, value, and tradition. Absolutely indestructible."

Like her, thought Joaquina, like her. She suddenly understood
the reason for the special consideration that Lorenza had shown
her for the last month. She also understood that Lorenza (who
was no fool) would not have dared ask her to lend the money.
"I would never lend it to her," she said, satisfied. "And she
knows it," she added to herself, becoming somber. "She knows
what I would do and what I wouldn't do for her. We know each
other too well. Her house . . . I can buy her house . . . I can do
something that she would never be able to do. Or at least not
now she can't. I can buy it and live . . . That would be the great-
est offense. To buy it and never permit her to come in. That
would be my vengeance. Vengeance for what?" The sentence
that had haunted her since last night came back: "If anything
happens, Joaquina, you are . . ." Where did that little fool get
the idea that she could scold her? Vengeance for that? No! She
was right. I shouldn't have . . . But why do I do these things?

"I am not interested."

"I cannot accept that answer. You are no fool. Get possession
of it. I'm not telling you to buy it to make a family museum.
You have outgrown that stage. But you are a practical woman.

And I'll swear to you that for any other buyer the price would be a quarter of a million pesos, but for you, since you are related to Lorenza Landero, the price is only two hundred thousand. A bargain! For Joaquina Coviella, of course. Buy it and make a hotel of it or an apartment house, whatever you want. But buy it!"

"Yes," she answered, speaking for her own benefit, "that's the way to look at the thing, the practical way. I would never be able to buy that property without thinking about its utilitarian value. It's true. You have come to offer me a bargain. The land alone is worth the two hundred thousand."

"Two hundred thousand pesos that for you are nothing."

"Nothing! Today is really your day, Saturnino."

She rested her head in her hand and thought about Hugo. A little after midnight Gabriel brought him back. Joaquina went out in the cold air and the heavy fog to take him by the feet and carry him to the sofa, where Lorenza was already waiting with a cup of hot coffee. He had a cut on his forehead very close to his right eyebrow. Joaquina reached out to take care of him and suddenly broke down into sobs, into screams. And she remembered that while she was calming herself she had seen the two young Coviella women: Esther with her handkerchief, weeping, away from them, Lorenza standing by the window smoking, loathing Joaquina.

"What is the final price, Saturnino?"

"Ah, Joaquina. Now I understand you completely, you are Sephardic too."

"Don't be stupid!"

"But we have identified each other. My ancestors . . ."

"Don't say any more about it! I know what that Sephardic business is all about. And it doesn't matter to me. Just tell me what the selling price is."

"They have given me a margin of ten thousand. I swear that's the truth, Joaquina. I can bring the owner right here to make you believe it. Ten thousand for me. We'll split. Five and five . . . A hundred and ninety five thousand for you, not a cent less."

"That is Lorenza's price," she said to herself. "I am worth

more, much more. My properties, the ones that don't even matter to me, are worth more. And for her the house is everything. She wants Eusebio to be a Landero, not a Coviella. But that's not important. It's not that. The child is worth it. He's a fine boy, almost a grandson to me . . . If I should ask her for him, if she should say to me . . . Idiot! No, it could never be."

"Saturnino, I am very sorry, but I am not interested."

Her tone disconcerted him. He looked at the small office, then at the window, through which he saw a landscape that was like an impressionistic sketch made vague by the fog, and then he looked again at Joaquina, serene, decisive.

"You don't mean that. If you can't decide today, perhaps tomorrow, whenever you wish. My client is not in a hurry. I will explain your doubts to him."

"I have no doubts. I don't want to buy the house."

"But that's impossible. Twenty years ago . . ."

"That's right. I don't deny it, Saturnino. Twenty years ago, but not today."

"Tomorrow."

"Never. Do you prefer cognac or sherry?"

"But what about Lorenza?"

"Cognac or sherry?"

"Cognac, please. I always tell Soledad"—he was speaking of his wife—"that a cognac in Las Vigas tastes better than in Jalapa. The cold, the altitude . . ."

"Rita," shouted Joaquina, standing in the doorway, "bring the cognac."

Joaquina took another sip and enjoyed thinking about how long it would be before she saw Saturnino Linares again. She sneezed several times and put the letter which she had already opened on her desk. It was absurd, utterly incomprehensible, that Lola Bárcena should have anything to do with this moment here in Las Vigas. She sneezed loudly and recalled the night mist, and Hugo's body . . . Then her memory turned again to Lola Bárcena, mixing the two lines of thought. Another sneeze. No, it was impossible. Still another sneeze. Lola Bárcena . . .

Joaquina recently married. Shy, poorly dressed, she clung to the deck rail, observing the boring, grayish-green sea, exactly the same as it was the day before. The noise of the waves, a continuous saying of something incomprehensible, the weak sun, the enormous sky. The idea sometimes that the earth is small, ephemeral, unstable, and that the only solid reality is water, the greenish gray, grayish green of the sea. And then, unexpectedly, a voice:

"What is your name?"

An angular, pretty woman was asking the question. And it was obvious that she really didn't care whether Joaquina told her or not, because, without even waiting, she said:

"I am Lola Bárcena."

"I . . . Joaquina Co . . . Señora Larragoitia."

"A newlywed! I might have guessed it. My face had the same . . ."

And that's the way her friendship with Lola Bárcena began. They saw each other constantly until they arrived in New York. Joaquina's first six months in America were spent there. And she lost contact with the first friend she made as a married woman. Lola had made friends with her through a combination of persistence and wit. Luis Larragoitia had lots of connections in New York and he could not go among his friends with an inadequate wife. So he educated her.

The memory of that period stayed alive in Joaquina's mind for many years. The constant lessons, the trips to the stores, the "being somebody" that depended on the way she dressed, the way she ate, the way she talked, the way she laughed . . . She learned rapidly, but she never stopped thinking of it as a game, a way to please the man who was her husband and whom she loved more and more. The sudden change from inhibitions and deprivations to the most expansive luxury and freedom did not change her basically. At those elegant dinners to which Luis took her, he was always whispering to her, "In Mexico it wouldn't be this way. It is different in Mexico. This is just a vacation." And she listened to his words without really hearing them. Just as she paid attention to his lessons. She could watch a naked woman dancing near them just as if she had done it every day in Asturias. She could pretend to enjoy the opera, the symphony, the gatherings where her ignorance of the language obliged her to express her approval, friendship, and intelligence with smiles and gestures. "Everyone says you are charming," Luis would say to her at night as he undressed her. "They say your laughter is wonderful." And she was incapable of believing it, yet at the same time was incapable of denying anything that he affirmed.

Later, in Jalapa, Lola Bárcena appeared again. To put it more accurately, she didn't appear, she was waiting for her.

"If it hadn't been for you, I would have killed myself. I've been waiting for you for ten days. My Francisco, the one I was going to marry, has disappeared."

Five years and five hundred unpaid pesos later, she came back one day.

"I know there is no excuse for it, dearie, I know it. I should have written you when Luis died, because although you didn't tell me about it, I found out from another Spanish girl. But I just couldn't. I don't know where time goes, it just disappears, dearie, it just disappears. And I'm embarrassed about not having paid you. Of course you don't need it..."

And after that, letters. A letter a year, and then a letter every two years: "If you could, please, things have gone badly for me..."

Then years and years passed without any news from her until today, in a letter from the Spanish Charities: "She says that you are her only friend in Mexico, that her maiden name is Dolores Bárcena." She immediately saw many pictures of her in her mind's eye. She heard her happy laugh, her jokes, she saw her wink. And Lola was there in her office that day. She made her think about Luis Larragoitia, about something—a woman—who no longer was or who never had come to be. She made her laugh, feel young...

Doña Teresa opened the office door.

"We are waiting for you to have dinner," she said.

"I am coming," Joaquina answered, standing up.

She smoothed her skirt, thinking about Lola Bárcena in a hospital bed that she couldn't pay for, about the sea, about a dark man—an Arabic type—kissing a young and gay Lola.

It was a silent meal. Everyone was waiting for Joaquina to tell them something interesting and she couldn't do it. She felt unhappy, alone, weak. Her eyes met the eyes of Lorenza, who was looking at her coldly, and then smiling she said:

"Saturnino came to talk about a business deal. He wants to sell me your house."

Lorenza blushed, looked at her eagerly, incapable of swallowing the bite that she had in her mouth.

"Of course, I told him that I wasn't interested."

chapter 10

"The dogs barked at the mist all night. Did they wake you up, señora?" Alejandro asked as he finished lighting the fire in the living room fireplace.

"Yes," Esther answered, getting close to the fire because she was so cold. "They woke me up several times." She almost touched the logs with her hands and still did not feel any warmth. "I'm frozen!"

It was early October and the whole region, caught in the grip of cold, foggy weather, sank into a gray and heavy lethargy. The cold, sharp as a knife, found its way through every crack around the doors and windows.

"They were barking at demons," Alejandro explained.

"At evil spirits," said Doña Teresa. She looked at herself in the big mirror. She was like a cadaver, dressed in black, with the beads of her rosary passing slowly over her fingers. "We must pray, Alejandro, we must go to church."

Esther felt afraid. She disliked this vision of her mother-in-law standing erect before the mirror like a statue. Doña Teresa had a habit of coming in without making any noise until she was just a step away, and then you could hear her murmuring endless prayers. She said that the cold weather kept her from praying sitting down and so she started wandering about the house, going from room to room, opening doors and not closing them. Esther thought her mother-in-law was going mad. "That's the way she gets every year, especially in October, near the anniversary of Papá's death," Gabriel explained.

The clock struck eleven times. Esther's hands were lukewarm now and she tried to bring life to her face by rubbing her skin. She turned on the light. It seemed impossible that it could be eleven o'clock in the morning. It was so dark it looked more like evening.

"Is something wrong, my dear? You look pale, sad."

"Nothing. I'm a little tired and cold."

"It's the time of year, señora. Take care of yourself," Alejandro said as he went out.

Esther pulled her clothing closer around her, covered her shoulders with a wool shawl, and looked for a comfortable seat on the sofa. The cat observed her and, as soon as Esther got settled, jumped up on her lap and began to rub against her, purring. Esther didn't want him to leave: she saw him, saw the fire, then saw the book that Lorenza had left behind, reached out and picked it up. *Murder For Beginners* was the title. She heard her mother-in-law go out, and sighed. She did feel depressed. She put the book down in favor of stroking the cat. She had thought she was pregnant until last night. Almost at dawn she felt a pain at her waist line and an hour later her period began. She wanted a child. Hugo wanted one too. Their belonging to each other was mutual, total. After the orgasm, Hugo would caress her placidly, and both of them, satisfied, would listen to the immense silence of the night, aware of the weak glow of the night light and speaking to each other in whispers. Short sentences that were more guessed than heard. Dreams, names for their child. "If it was today, he will be born in June." At first they had thought their child would be born in March, and now not even in June. When would it be? Would it ever really be? What month?

Joaquina came in.

"Did you keep on?" she asked.

"Yes . . ."

After throwing some more wood on the fire, Joaquina sat down in one of the armchairs.

"Try not to worry about it. You are both very young and have lots of time. Many years for many children." She sighed. "I know it's depressing because in these first months one always wants a child. I wanted one so much!"

Yes, day in and day out she had longed for a child, to complete her love for Luis Larragoitia. She imagined that they would live years and years together and she knew that she had married him without loving him and that she ought to compensate by establishing other ties. But even without a child she came to love him and gladly accepted his pampering and his passion. Sometimes at night she remembered the contact with his slim body, the warm and hairy skin, the desire ultimately shared in long kisses that one day, still unsatisfied, had ceased. She took off the sheets that were damp with sweat and began to dress the slender body before it became rigid—without a tear, incapable of understanding death, there before the first dead person she had ever seen. She understood it the day after, when she went to bed alone, a bed that would never again be warmed by any body but her own, the widow of Luis Larragoitia. The funeral expenses made her aware for the first time of numbers, pesos, payments, costs. Later on she became accustomed to business affairs and was praised for it. "You were born to be a business woman." "Not even your husband would have made such a good deal." She soon realized that her brother Eusebio was no help at all; and if she didn't want them to rob her, she herself would have to take charge of the innumerable enterprises that her husband had run. Luis Larragoitia had an import agency in Veracruz and was one of the nation's principal importers. He also had coffee and orange plantations, and considerable wealth in the form of real estate and cash. "But you can't sell the import agency, that's what produces most of the income," Eusebio explained. "And who is going to run it, who *can* run it?" Her brother immediately said that he could, and Joaquina laughed aloud. "I don't want to lose a cent. We will sell now while the business is in good shape, not when it is bankrupt." And to the astonishment of her fellow Spaniards, she began to sell and then to buy land, houses, and farms, with the disapproval of everyone who knew about it. By the time she was thirty years old (five years later) she was very rich. She did receive proposals of marriage, but not one could convince her that her physical charms were the first consideration. When she told Lola Bárcena about it, her friend reproached her for underestimating herself. "And what about your body? Don't tell me fairy tales. Do you have a lover? The Andalusian who was here yesterday, don't you have anything going with him?" "No, not with anybody." "Well, dearie, I just can't understand you. He's a real charmer. I know you were happy with Luis, but any way you look at it, it was a short happiness. Don't you feel empty? Don't you feel that you need someone?" Yes, I feel that I need someone, she said to herself that day. A week later Lola Bárcena again disappeared from Jalapa. The note she left behind said, "I am going away with the Andalusian." Yes, I need someone, she kept on thinking month after month. She lived with her brother and Teresa, without envying their love, because they seemed silly and superficial to her. She did envy them when Hugo was going to be born. She attended her sister-in-law, took care of her, and looked out for her with a concern that astonished them. And on the night the baby came, she said to her brother: "I have never asked you for anything and I have helped you as much as I could. Now I want something: I want Hugo to be mine. Give him to me! I'll pay you anything you want!" "But Joaquina, that's impossible. How do you think that we . . . My children are yours, your nephews, both of them. But give him to you, no . . . no . . . " Lola Bárcena came back to Jalapa with welts all over her back; and after she had told Joaquina who had beaten her and why, she learned about Joaquina's wanting a child and burst out laughing: "You ninny! If you want a child, let somebody make one for you. That's a favor that's never denied anybody with a face like yours. And if you don't want it that way, honey, let me do it in your place. Just tell me who you want to be the father." And she kept on laughing while Joaquina took care of her wounds, and she caught the mood too and they laughed together for a long time . . . Now she smiled. How could I forget Lola? Poor thing, she must be an old woman. I am going to see her. It's hard to see how these last years have passed without my thinking of her even once. I'll bring her here to live . . .

"Here's coffee, would you like some?" Lorenza asked, coming in with the tray and cups.

"Please," both of them answered.

Lorenza gave each a cup, poked the fire, and sat down near Esther.

"This is the best thing about Las Vigas," she said, "these days, and this cold when the fireplace is burning brightly."

"It's like winter in Spain," Joaquina said, "with fewer inconveniences, but much like this. All the aunts and uncles, cousins, friends, and neighbors used to get together to chat a while, telling stories about winter, things that had happened, things they had heard about. We children would listen for hours and hours. Sometimes it makes me want to go back."

"I've never been able to understand why you haven't gone," Lorenza said. "I'd have gone back a long time ago."

"You know I didn't get along very well with my family, especially with my father. But now I'd like to go back. I'd like to take a friend, Lola Bárcena, with me. She hasn't been back either, since the time we came together. Now she's in a hospital, sick. Maybe next year. Summer is the best time."

"It's the worst time in Cuernavaca," Esther said. She smiled, remembering a happy day. "Lots of tourists, too hot . . . The nights are beautiful, with fiestas by the side of the pool."

"I'm freezing," Doña Teresa said when she came in. "It gets colder every year! I told Cristóbal to take care of the dogs and to let Burgos come in here. We old people suffer more from the cold. You shouldn't let Eusebio play outside in weather like this, Lorenza. It might make him sick."

"I know it, but that's where he's happy. He didn't sleep well last night because the dogs kept waking him up. Did you hear them?"

"Why do you suppose they were barking? Do you think someone was trying to get in?" Esther asked.

Doña Teresa served herself some coffee, but then went to

look for the cognac because she needed a few drops. When she came back Burgos was following her, trembling and looking happy. He came over to lick Lorenza's hand and then he lay down at her feet, on top of her shoes.

"No, nobody bothers us. Well, yes, sometimes they do rob us, but not very much. When I bought this house they told me it was a piece of foolishness, that nobody would be able to live peacefully in this place where the people are evil and dangerous. But I have never been afraid during all the time we have lived here, and they also say there are ghosts who have killed I don't know how many people."

"Unfortunately, ghosts are a European privilege," Lorenza said. "I would like to see one sometime. Maybe in my house." She stopped talking, blushed, and her eyes met Joaquina's. "Anyway, I like to believe those things."

"Good heavens, child, what a taste! Don't talk to me about ghosts. It is the devil, it is evil . . ."

"If you believe such things, I don't understand why you are always reading detective stories. Don't they make you afraid?"

"Oh, no, not at all! You see, I really don't think . . . I don't really believe, but I enjoy it a lot. Sometimes I find out who the murderer is or who the murderer is going to be, and that is fascinating. It makes you think, and you start examining each one of the characters, studying his motives, his capacity for murder."

"Lorenza!" Doña Teresa exclaimed. "You know I don't like you to talk about such things!"

"Of course, not all of them commit murder," Lorenza kept on without paying attention to her mother-in-law. "And as a matter of fact, sometimes we readers are bloodier than the characters. We find more plausible motives, more opportunities for killing without being punished. There are so many complicated and subtle ways of killing . . ."

"Lorenza, please! If you keep on, my coffee is going to turn bitter."

"Speak to your mother-in-law only of prayers and priests," Joaquina said.

"I don't like to talk about it either," Esther said.

"No, for the love of God. No, for the love of God," murmured Doña Teresa, making the sign of the cross.

"It doesn't seem like midday," Joaquina said.

"It's so thick and dark outside, it looks as if the whole world has stopped existing."

"Yes, it's so dark I had to turn the light on a little while ago."

"Now I'm waiting for a ghost to come out of the clock," Lorenza said.

"The phantom of the hours," Esther said, smiling. "With seven eyes, two noses, and twenty tails."

"And speaking another language," Lorenza said.

"The phantom of time," Doña Teresa said.

"And the phantom of times! Times of joy, times of tribulation, times of sadness, of sickness, and of health," Joaquina exclaimed, laughing.

"Times of sadness. Soon it will be seven years since Eusebio died. You never knew him, Esther, you never saw his eyes."

A gust of arctic air touched them, then immediately they heard the laughter and the running feet of Eusebio. "Mamá! Mamá! The black dog had puppies."

chapter 11

One, two, three! One, two, three! One, two, three! Onetwo-three! The boys were marching erect, although somewhat irregularly, through the fog.

"Who are they?" Eusebio asked, clutching the balcony rail at his Aunt Amelia's while he imitated the rhythm of the march.

"Some explorers who are going to the country," Gabriel explained.

"They're children," Eusebio said, still imitating their rhythm.

"Yes," Gabriel answered. He turned to Hugo. "It used to be a daily thing at school. Remember? Well, as a matter of fact, you don't remember. We used to march every day. Tuesdays we would go to throw stones at churches, Thursdays at saloons. Fridays we always saw Russian films that featured inordinately healthy women who looked energetic and wore uniforms and carried rifles. It frightened me to think that Mamá might dress that way. I didn't want life to be a battlefield, much less have Mamá connected in some way with a weapon. To a certain extent, I feel the same repugnance now toward these boy scouts."

Tuesdays, one two three, to the church. They stopped them on the cathedral steps. The teacher, Francisco Lagos, made a speech to convince them again (he did it three times a day at least) that Catholicism, the Church, and the priest were pernicious and execrable. Gabriel loved his teacher, loved his hard face, his mouth, which was the source of solemn words, phrases full of fire and sincerity. He loved him more than he loved Don

Eusebio, who knew nothing of the Mexican Revolution, who had never taken part in any struggle in this country. Gabriel accepted all of his teacher's orders and opinions; he wrote his anticlerical compositions, and with great pride accepted the prize he won: a word of praise, a good grade . . . Señor Lagos decided to form a cooperative, or more exactly, a savings box. Each child would bring five centavos a week and at the end of the year, after classes were over, they would divide up the savings. Monday was collection day and Gabriel was the one elected to collect it. As the months passed, this Monday tribute turned into a custom like lots of others and the children stopped thinking about how much money there was and how the project would turn out. The school was very old, on the point of falling down, and the government undertook some repairs that consisted principally of reinforcing the stairway that went to the second floor—the girls' floor—and fixing up the rooms that were in the worst condition. They bought sand, cement, and bricks, and for lack of a better place to put them, they ended up in the patio where the boys played their games. This obliged the teachers to send the boys to the central garden where the girls played. There Gabriel could see Lorenza during recess and participate in the general admiration that she aroused among all the boys. When classes were over, after examinations, Señor Lagos reminded them of their savings. He explained ahead of time that not all the children had contributed as regularly as they should have. However, their lack of cooperation, although it meant that there wasn't as much capital as there might have been, did not mean that some were going to receive more and others less. Everyone would receive the same amount. But before distributing the money, he wanted to ask them a favor. He also had a little reconstruction job at his house. He was repairing the dining room and building a chicken house, and since they had brought more bricks than were needed to repair the school, he wanted the boys to take some over to his house— twenty per boy. When each one had fulfilled his obligation he would receive his share of the savings. They heard the request with shouts of glee and went to work like ants. Señor Lagos lived about seven blocks from the school. It was a very short walk, but carrying the bricks made it infinitely longer. Gabriel and almost all of his companions had to make more than five trips in order to fulfill the quota. The job took all morning and Gabriel felt the need of going to the bathroom. When he saw the teacher's wife he told her so and she showed him where the bathroom was. They passed through the dining room and then went into a small room almost completely filled by a double bed. Gabriel took it all in and saw an enormous "Heart of Jesus" at the head of the bed. He knew the picture because his mother had a small one in her bedroom. But it did not seem possible that Señor Lagos would have one too. Beyond any doubt it was a whim of his wife's, something she had insisted on . . . Or had he lied? Had he deceived them? He didn't find out and he didn't want to think about it. Emotionless, he received a fifty centavo coin from the hand of Señor Lagos, who patted his head when he gave him the money. Gabriel did not say thank you but went alone to the nearby park with the disagreeable sensation that he had been deceived.

"Three, three, three," said Eusebio, jumping. "They're going away, Papá, where are you going?"

"To the country, I told you."

"Three, three . . . Let's go with them."

"Come on, I'll take you," Hugo said, taking him by the hand.

Gabriel kept on observing the street, the automobiles that were passing, the people. It was cold and the fog was beginning to descend, although it was not as heavy as it had been in Las Vigas when they left.

"Here he is," Esther shouted, looking outside. "They were asking if you had left." She leaned against the balcony. "The city is pretty. I used to think it was like Cuernavaca."

"No, it's much prettier."

"Provincial . . . Come in, Lorenza's aunt wants to offer you some whisky."

Lorenza was playing scales on the piano. Aunt Amelia, dressed in gray silk, perfectly coiffured, received him with a glass tinkling with ice.

"I was telling him that he is provincial," Esther said.

"No, my child, the province no longer exists, because the speed of traveling from one place to another has abolished it. Now we are inaccurate, grotesque reproductions of the capital, and the capital is an inaccurate and grotesque reproduction of Paris, of New York, or of any other large city. Because we have imitated others, we have lost the purity of the province . . . It used to be different, my dear."

"Now she's going to drag out every Landero since the Flood," Lorenza said.

"The only thing they still haven't taken from us is the country. From that point of view Jalapa is still provincial and that's why people live happily here. We live surrounded by trees, hills, and gardens. The greenness is what makes our city beautiful, what gives it life. It's the only worthwhile thing we have left from the old days. When I was in exile it was what I remembered most, what I missed most, not seeing this greenness washed clean by the rain, not seeing the sunsets, luminous beyond reality, that come after a heavy shower. I could do without the people, but not without the other things. Here now in this city that is no longer my city—invaded as it is by newcomers who think that political posts can make up for what they lack in background, in breeding, and in distinction—the only thing that consoles me is that these things I love most cannot be spoiled. They have already spoiled the rest: the Casino, the old houses, the haciendas that now belong to the newly rich. Even names have lost their value, or have disappeared. The people who have stayed here are very few and even fewer of us have come back. A distant relative of mine was trying to persuade me to sell this house and come to live in Mexico in Las Lomas. As if that could ever be as distinguished as the provinces. It is absurd, as absurd as thinking of building a modern house here in Jalapa. And still there are people who are proud of their new houses. No! No! It is death. The old families used to know how to conserve tradition. We lived well, had good taste—not only the Landeros . . ."

And Doña Amelia, to Lorenza's delight, began to speak of the

Landero family, and kept on until Gabriel interrupted to say that if Lorenza was going to take Eusebio to the doctor, they had better leave.

When they came out of the doctor's office the cathedral clock struck two. Eusebio was in excellent condition: "A little thin, perhaps, but very tall for his age. He could use a few vitamins." The fog had invaded the city. They were going toward the downtown area at the hour when the shops were closed. The mist pushed up against the shop windows, dampening them. Two small, elderly ladies, elegantly dressed in black, greeted Lorenza.

"They must be waiting for us at the Casino. Would you like to see my house?" Lorenza asked, and Esther said she would. "Then let's go by on the way," and she continued what she had been telling. "In those days we almost lived on charity, thanks to the fact that the merchants had sold to our family for twenty or thirty years and we still had a good reputation. So they trusted us for everything from clothing to meat. The funny thing is that I was surrounded by poverty and privations without noticing it. I was never aware of my parents' difficulties, never knew when they could or couldn't pay what they owed. I always knew, of course, that there were certain troubles, that Papá's illness was a serious one, and that a lot of money was going for medicine with no income to make up for it—we were living with the help of my aunt—but Mamá never talked about their trouble. I found out for myself, little by little, in elementary school. What kept up the lie, fortunately for me, was the political change. There were no private schools and all the girls, rich and poor, went to public school. Later on I entered secondary school but I was there only for the first year. Aunt Amelia came to visit us and said that it wasn't necessary to exhibit our poverty. Her husband had just died and she took us to Puebla to live with her. I dreaded going to another city to live and I dreaded even more being the poor relative. But Aunt Amelia is a real charm and she treated me like a princess, showering me with clothing and attentions of all kinds, hiring private tutors so my education would be 'equal to that of all the Landeros.' Mamá died when I was sixteen years old and from that time on I was Aunt Amelia's daughter and she took charge of my future. She bought one of the houses that had belonged to the Landeros— the one she lives in now—and had it repaired and furnished for me, for the two of us. We kept on living in Puebla for several years because she had business dealings there, but we spent different periods of time here—the end of the summer for the grand ball at the Casino, and the Christmas posadas, Christmas itself, and New Year. I had a different suitor each year, to my delight. But I didn't fall in love with any of them. Now, romantically, it consoles me and pleases me to think that I was waiting for Gabriel, whom I always loved, whom I had liked since elementary school. I was married when I was twenty-seven and since then I've been buying things for my great-grandparents' house so I can live there someday as they did. And I hope that a child of mine will be born in that house. Now you are going to see it, although it will only be from the outside. For me, of course, it's the finest house in the world."

She was walking rapidly, spurred on by her words. The mist was so heavy, you could hardly see three feet ahead.

"It's in this block at the end of the street."

Esther saw that the line of houses came to an end and then there was some rubbish in an enormous open space. A group of stonemasons were eating, seated on a pile of stones. Lorenza dropped Eusebio's hand and began to walk faster. For the first time in her life her eyes could see the area that had always been in her dreams. She began to run among the stones, stepping on this place for the first time, and came up to the group of men.

"What are you doing? What has happened? Where is the house that belongs here?"

"They're going to build a movie theater, a big one. The best in the city."

chapter 12

Eusebio woke up before anyone called him. His room was in
shadow as he sat up in bed and looked about the walls, search-
ing for something new: a toy, a gift. There was something
special about today, something that had made him wake up
early. He dreamed that he was at El Bordo, that his Uncle Hugo
and Aunt Esther had taken him there again, and that they were
all walking along together looking for squirrels' nests. They
went into the woods, led on by the promise that Hugo knew the
place where they could find them. Accustomed to the darkness,
Eusebio could see the walls clearly. There was nothing new:
the soldiers, the bear, the conch shells and the colored rocks,
the savings bank that had broken a few days ago because he
tried to play ball with it . . . He heard some noise in his parents'
bedroom and then he heard Burgos' bark. Papá says that when
the puppies are bigger I can play with them, that if I carry them
around now I may drop them and kill them. Francisco and Alejandro kill lambs, and calves too. Men know how to kill. When
I'm bigger I'll learn too. My Uncle Hugo didn't find the squirrels. Cristóbal is going to build me a trap like his for hunting
rabbits. I really don't like rabbits because they bite. One day
Rita brought one to the kitchen—a white one with red eyes.
"Let me have it, Rita, give him to me." "No, it'll get away from
you and it's for dinner." "Are you going to kill it?" Rita gave

him the rabbit and when Eusebio tried to pat it, the rabbit bit his finger. Squirrels are better, with a longer and prettier tail, and they don't bite children. He looked at the chair and on it saw his dress-up suit, black wool with white buttons. A fiesta! He didn't remember what fiesta, but the proof was there: leather shoes, silk shirt . . . Suddenly he remembered and quickly jumped to the floor.

"Mamá! Mamá! Wake up, dress me. I'm going to Puebla with Aunt Joaquina."

He saw her already standing there, smiling and wearing her blue bathrobe that came to the floor.

"Don't walk around in your bare feet, you'll get sick."

"Get me dressed, Mamá! Get me dressed!"

"Aren't you cold?" Gabriel asked.

He saw him, laughed with him, and shook his head while his mother picked him up and put him in bed with them.

"Why are you in bed?"

"It's Sunday."

"I'm going to Puebla with Aunt Joaquina."

While Lorenza went to get his clothes, Eusebio started to jump around and fell over Gabriel, almost on his face. He put his hands on his father's cheeks. The rough contact pleased him.

"When I'm big will I have a beard?"

"Yes."

"It's like a hairbrush . . . My Uncle Hugo took me to hunt squirrels."

"Is that right? When?"

"The other day, yesterday. We didn't find any. They hide but he knows where their house is and he's going to take me and we're going to hunt a lot of them. A lot of them! Squirrels are nice and love children, and they have houses and they have papás."

"Have you seen their houses?"

"Yes."

They dressed him and he went out running, climbed the winding stairs, and came to the hallway. Rita said good morn-

ing to him, but he didn't pay any attention to her and kept on
running till he arrived at Aunt Joaquina's room to wake her up.

The music, tropical, rhythmic . . . He lit a cigarette and with
it described in the air the imaginary movements of an orchestra
conductor. He accompanied the movements with a clicking of
fingers.

"Wake up."

"No. It's Sunday."

"You're already awake, open your eyes."

"No, it's too cold. Let me alone. Turn off that radio."

"I'm cold too."

"Put on your pajamas."

"It's time to get up."

"No, Hugo, don't wake me up! Go to sleep," she told him,
laughing and touching his lips.

"Tum tum te tum! Tum tum te tum! Te tum! What rhythm
is that?"

"I don't know."

"You knew when you were in Cuernavaca."

"You're crazy. It's so cold!"

"You said you were going to like the cold. Get up, lazybones,
I'm lazy enough for both of us. Tum tum te tum te tum! Joaquina is going to Puebla! Joaquina is going to Puebla!" He said
the sentence in rhythm with the melody. "We're going to be
here alone, we're going to be here alone!"

"That's right! Let's have breakfast!"

The two of them got out of bed. Esther grabbed her clothes
and, trembling with cold, hurriedly took off her nightgown and
began to dress as fast as she could. Hugo continued his dance.

"Aren't you getting cold that way?"

"I'm in heat."

"You'd better be in your clothes. What do you want for breakfast?"

"Lobster with white wine. Tum tum te tum te tum!"

"Sundays affect you."

"Joaquina's trips affect me. Tum te tum!"

She left him while he was putting on his shorts, doing a balancing act and still dancing.

"He was not drunk, O God, you know well he was not drunk. It was a heart attack. Seven years ago today." After the outburst she finished the prayer. "Holy Mary, Mother of God, pray for him and for us sinners now and at the hour of our death. Amen."

She buttoned the dress up to her neck and looked at herself. Her hair was completely white, her face the color of wax. Its skin seemed to get thinner and thinner and more tightly stretched over the bones. Only her eyes seemed alive—in them there was a little of the light she had shared with Eusebio. It would grieve him to see me this way. But he'll never see me at all. Never! We used to take walks every Sunday, around Los Berros and the stadium. And all the women we met used to be envious because he was so handsome. They would have taken him away from me if they could. But he would take my hand and tell me all about Asturias and wouldn't even notice those hussies. I was the only one he saw . . . And he'd spend hours looking at me, telling me how pretty I was. I was envious of the years before I knew him, wishing we could recapture the time we hadn't been able to share. He used to go trout fishing in the river, swim with his cousins in the ice cold mountain streams . . . When he was ten or twelve years old. He must have been wonderful. I don't know how I happened to be the lucky one. So many other girls were prettier. Joaquina told me so one day, and she told me ugly things about him too. But Eusebio didn't care. He acted as if he didn't even hear me talking about it. "Forget about other people. You and I are the only ones who matter." And he was so happy when he found out I was pregnant. He brought me pistachios, dried fruit, cheese. "Do you want anything special? What would you like?" Neither of the boys turned out to be as thoughtful as he was. He would lie down close to me, using my legs for a pillow, and ask me to scratch his head. I don't think it was so terrible that he took a few drinks now and then. I never quarreled with him about it, and I told Joaquina that she shouldn't either. And anyway, if anybody did any quarreling, it ought to be me. But how could I fuss with him? He would just act even more loving and say things to me and start to laugh that happy laugh of his. Why did he die? Why didn't I go first, or the two of us together?

But the mirror gave no answer, so she wiped away a tear and smoothed her gray hair. The rheumatism pain hurt her back and she moaned. When, when will God take me where he is?

"I won't be able to go to Mass," she said aloud. "It's hurting more than it did yesterday. I will pray for you here. It amounts to the same thing."

She opened her door.

Joaquina shouted:

"All right, all right, wait a minute!"

She finished combing her hair and opened the door for the child.

"Is it time to go?"

"We're going to eat breakfast first. Aren't you cold?"

"No, but Mamá says I'm going to wear my overcoat."

She took him by the hand and they went out.

"Come with me," Joaquina said.

They crossed the living room, went into the entrance hall, ran the bolts, and took away the bar. The air was frigid outside, the wind sharp, a pain in the ears.

"Look, Aunt Joaquina, the grass is hard."

"It froze last night. Walk carefully so you don't fall. That lazy Alejandro must be sleeping. Let's wake him up."

"Where do the other men sleep?"

"In their houses."

"Cristóbal lives with an old woman."

"Who told you that?"

"Lucio and Francisco. They said she was a dirty old woman and . . ."

"Don't you pay attention to what they say."

"Why not?"

"Because I say not."

"Oh! Mamá says . . . Look, there's Alejandro! Alejandro, Alejandro!"

He let go of Joaquina's hand and started running toward the man. But on the way he saw his cat, who hid when he heard the noise of footsteps. "Don't run, Kitty." He started running after him without hearing what Aunt Joaquina was saying to his back.

"I . . . I . . . Wait for me," he shouted, running down the hill after the cat.

If only they didn't spoil him so much, thought Joaquina, looking at him. In two years we will send him to a boarding school. She felt that the cold was making her ears and hands weigh more. Mist covered the treetops, clouding the landscape.

"Good morning, ma'am."

"Good morning. I'm leaving in a little while. You go to the pasture and tell Liborio that I'm not coming and that later on I'll see what he's done. But be sure you tell him, because if you don't, he'll go to town and get drunk. He still has a lot of work to do, and if it's not done by tomorrow it will be your fault."

She returned to the house feeling a happy little warmth, the happiness of going to see Lola.

Breakfast was quick. The bus went through town at eight in the morning and they had to be there a few minutes early.

"Yes," Esther answered, "he's up, but he'll have breakfast later."

Doña Teresa kissed first Joaquina and then Eusebio and said she was going to go to her room and stay there. No one asked her why because they all knew what day it was. She walked rapidly, taking her rosary from her pocket. The music reached her ears. It was an incomprehensible and revolting noise in English. Hugo was dancing in the living room.

"But, my child, that music! What are you doing?"

"I'm getting rid of the cold."

"But today? Today! Don't you remember what day this is?"

"Look at this step . . ."

"Hugo, go have your breakfast. Your father died seven years ago today. Please, please, turn off that radio."

He paid no attention to her and she herself went into the bedroom and turned it off.

"Where is Puebla?" Eusebio asked.

"It's a city. We'll be there in three hours."

Hugo stopped the car when they got to the park. In spite of the fact that it was Sunday—a market day—there was no one to be seen. The cold was intense, the fog descended lower and lower. A few seconds later the bus appeared. Hugo opened the automobile door so his aunt could get out, and helped her climb into the other vehicle. Eusebio had already gone ahead of them, happy about the adventure.

Since there were no other passengers, the bus left immediately. Hugo stood there in the highway, shivering.

He went back to the car, saw another bus coming from the other direction on its way to Jalapa, to Veracruz. The engine was hard to start. He watched some women coming out of church, trembling with cold, almost completely covered by their rebozos. Then he turned on the radio as loud as it would go and began to sing. He felt free and happy. He ought to take advantage of Aunt Joaquina's trip and make something special of the day. "But what?" he asked himself as he drove toward the house. The fog was very thick. He kept on singing but the song sounded strange, out of place, in that damp, depressing landscape—a shrouded, dead landscape, a landscape of silence and indestructible immensity, incapable of communicating joy. If only there were a little color, just a little. But there would be none for the next four months. Every day they would be herded together and cut off from the world by the fog. With or without Joaquina the place was not going to change. It couldn't become joyful, noisy, vibrant with light, color, and pleasure.

Suddenly he began to laugh. Then his laughter grew louder and became pure joy. He stopped the car in front of the house and went in laughing, jumping.

"Let's go! Right now! Let's go to the coast where it's warm. We can be there in two hours. Come on, come on. Let's go to Veracruz."

chapter 13

"No, Hugo! Don't!" she cried as she saw him approaching.

She wanted to get away, but he grabbed her by the ankles and eliminated any possibility of escape, submerging her at the same time. She swallowed a little salt water, stretched out her arms and kicked. Now she was free again. When she came up the sun blinded her. Then she heard Hugo's roar of laughter and saw his eyes sparkle, made almost green by the sea.

"You look like a frightened child!" he said, laughing, then swam away from her rapidly.

Esther spat and swam after him, but Hugo left her farther behind with each stroke. The joke-scare made her feel uncertain and she lost her bearings. Suddenly a monstrous sea appeared before her. She thought that the waves were carrying her away, that she was getting lost, that death was there. She tried to go back, to escape as fast as she could, but a large wave washed over her, and she lost all sense of direction. She blinked. Water came into her eyes, her mouth, and then she felt something encircle her waist. She didn't cry out because she was afraid she might swallow more water. Then she felt the air, a red light struck her eyes, and she opened them. She saw Lorenza and Gabriel laughing and suddenly she came out of the water on the way to the sky in her husband's arms.

"The champion swimmer, and her husband, the champion lifeguard!"

She held on to his neck, hid her face against him. Her eyes

were a fraction of an inch from Hugo's nipple. She closed them and bit her lips so the others wouldn't know that she had really thought she was drowning, that she didn't want to die, that she had been afraid, very afraid . . . She opened her eyes again when she sensed that her husband's footsteps were more secure. She put her cheek close to his, dried her tears on him as if it were a caress. Then she saw the sea wall, the gray cement on top of which all the onlookers were standing—and above their heads the houses of the boulevard, the roof gardens, the tops of the palm trees, and over all of them the intensely blue sky of a color and warmth that were incomprehensible in the Coviella house.

"Hugo, kiss me."

They kissed.

"What happened is that you got tired. You've been swimming more than two hours."

He put her down on the sand. Esther combed her hair with the fingers of both hands. Some children were covering their father with sand. She laughed, remembering a joke from one of Hans Meyer's magazines. "It's the unconscious desire to bury their parents," Hans had said.

"You feel all right?" Lorenza asked her.

"Yes." She looked at her and thought that she was beautiful, that undoubtedly Lorenza was the most beautiful woman on the beach at that time.

"Are you sure?" Gabriel asked.

"Yes, Gabriel, I am sure, thank you. I swallowed a little water and got excited about it, but it's all over now."

"Okay, it's all over," Hugo exclaimed. "Now let's get dressed."

They ran off among hundreds of bathers.

"It certainly doesn't seem like winter is almost here," said a fat, dark woman dressed in a bathing suit.

"You're so tan."

"She's naturally tan," Hugo whispered.

The four of them laughed. From time to time a gust of cold air came down and swept across the beach, but it passed rapidly and the sun's rays were even more welcome than before.

They separated in the shade of the passageway between the

dressing rooms. Hugo and Gabriel went to the showers. Gabriel hesitated a few minutes, then turned on the water. It fell over his head, on his back, on his chest and slid over his whole body —not cold, almost lukewarm. He took pleasure in breathing, tasted salt on his lips, rubbed his cheeks, then took off his trunks and felt the direct contact of the drops of water on his belly and penis.

"Get out!" Hugo shouted, slapping him on the behind.

The blow left his skin burning, made a red mark on its naturally white color. He saw Hugo laughing and handing him the soap. He rubbed his skin energetically. The soap that dripped from his wet hair made him blink. He saw his brother's body, his gestures, and pushed him so he could get under the shower again to relieve the stinging in his right eye. Hugo stuck a finger in his ribs, laughed and shouted again until he got him from under the shower. Hugo's body—reddish, almost brown—was jumping about in front of him. It was strange that the difference in temperature should make them so different, so happy, so exactly themselves. It made him happy and nostalgic to see the agility and to hear the laughter of his brother. He was like a little boy again. Little Hugo, he thought, my little Hugo.

While they were putting on their clothes in the narrow little dressing room, they felt cold, but the warmth came back when they went out to the corridor. They waited for their wives at the entrance, looking at the bathers all gathered together in a few yards of sea and sand. Far away, almost on the horizon, there was a ship coming in—or was it going out? The sky cut by gulls was the same clear blue into the infinite distance, the undulating, inexact distance of the sea. Its immensity was absolute, indestructible.

The waiter pointed out an empty table at one end of the large room. They advanced among the dancing couples, zigzagging, stopping, until they finally got to the place they wanted. They sat down in uncomfortable wooden chairs near the wall that was next to the sea.

"We'll get drunk as a sacrifice to the sun," Hugo exclaimed.

"For you it will be no sacrifice," Lorenza replied, laughing. "But I approve of it because I've never been drunk. Right, Gabriel? Maybe I'll do it today."

"Neither have I," Esther said.

"Virtuous Mexican womanhood," Gabriel commented, pretending to look stern.

They drank several beers.

It was beginning to get cold.

The noise was unbearable. Gabriel suggested that it might be better to go to the *Portales*.

Hugo drove at an excessive speed along the boulevard. He screeched around curves, attracting everybody's attention. People turned around and looked at them disapprovingly. They were speeding toward the shore, intoxicated by the beer, by the intense colors, by the music on the radio. They reached the docks. Hugo pressed down on the horn to make people get out of their way.

"Quiet! Come on, cut that out!"

But instead of stopping, he kept right on blowing the horn, attracting attention, laughing. He was suddenly happy, suddenly blinded by the rays and reflections of the sun, which made him blink, and he had to slow down. He rubbed his eyes and kept going. The four of them were victims of a kind of subconscious eroticism caused by the light clothing worn by the people who lived there, by their spontaneous laughter, their languid movements, their irresponsible appearance. It was as if they had suddenly discovered what is positive about life and (since they hadn't known about it before) decided to fix everything up immediately. To go to the most extreme of extremes, no matter what. But to be happy, to laugh, to be like these sailors, these stevedores, to have the same sing-song voice— exaggerated, funny. They saw a man urinating in the middle of the street. His wife (surely it must be his wife) was holding him up by the arm. And they burst out laughing.

"Please be quiet, Hugo. They will throw us in jail."

"If they let people urinate right in the public street, I don't see why they would stop anybody from blowing an automobile horn."

At last they were downtown. They left the car beside the park and looked for a place in the *Portales*.

The marimbas were deafening, four or five of them playing different pieces at the same time.

"The noise here is worse!" Lorenza shouted.

"What?"

"The racket."

"Yes, it's wonderful! Dance, kid, dance!"

"Hugo . . ."

"I love you all, I adore all three of you. You are very dear to me." And before they could sit down he quickly kissed each of them.

Several other people arrived at the same time as the waiter: a vendor of cheap Italian jewelry, a woman selling tickets for the national lottery, and a half-naked child, dirty and smiling, who was collecting money for the marimba.

"A bottle of Scotch whisky to be opened here," Hugo shouted. "And a bottle of cold soda."

"That's a lot," Esther murmured when the waiter left.

"No, it isn't, beautiful. I'm still conscious. Later on, when I don't know what's going on, tell me it's too much. It's just a little to get us started. We haven't had anything to drink but some beer."

"Do you like them?"

"They're fake."

"Pardon?"

"The bracelets, the necklaces."

"Don't buy anything. It's cheaper in . . ."

"Would you like to help the marimba?"

"Today's prize, a half million, today's prize . . ."

"Woman, you're either drunk or crazy. There's no lottery today."

"I forgot." She burst out laughing. "What a fool! Tomorrow's prize . . ."

"What piece would you like?"

"We haven't been here for years."

"Look at that woman with the yellow scarf."

Lorenza looked. She was surely Scandinavian. The color of the scarf blended with the color of her hair. She was drinking with two equally blond sailors. The girl was exaggeratedly attractive, with a charming smile. Lorenza lit a cigarette and stared at the lottery tickets. No. Her house no longer existed. What good was money? *I don't care what other people say, I'm gonna spend my life without worryin' about nothin'. I don't care what other people say, I'm gonna spend my life without worryin' about nothin'.* She saw the white teeth of the singers, a noisy chorus needlessly emphatic—gesticulating, jumping around, and grinning. The sunny plaza was empty. Her cigarette smoke (she imagined it) rose through the foliage of an orange tree, went from there in diagonal ascent to the top of a palm, and then straight ahead until it stopped, turned into nothing, at the white wall of the church. The blonde screamed.

"Here's to us! Drink up! Drink up!"

"Make love to me, gorgeous, make love to me."

"Is all this a dream?"

"Ask them to play something Italian."

"Not yet, this isn't the moment."

A big basket full of shrimp. The vendor put it right under Gabriel's nose and he shoved it away. But the man was used to that. He moved it a few inches and left it there. Then he reached in and took out a few of the shrimp to show what good quality they were and how cheap he was selling them. Five beautiful shrimp, orange-red-white, jumped in his hand as he shook them to the rhythm of the marimba.

"Five pesos a dozen."

"Not interested."

"They're stupid, aren't they? If anyone else comes to sell something, don't pay any attention to him, please. Now, here's to us! Esther, I said here's to us!"

"Cheers! I want something Italian."

"No."

"Fresh shrimp! Fresh shrimp!"

"They should have a fan for each table."

"It was cold down by the sea."

"Winter's coming soon."

"Not here, thank heaven."

"Here's to Aunt Joaquina."

"Why?"

"Forget her!"

"Forget me?"

"Don't pay any attention to her. Shoot her."

"You're so gentle, Hugo. You really move me. Let's face it, the best thing is for them to shoot us all together."

"The check will kill us."

"Tightwad."

"I wonder what Eusebio is doing right now."

"I wonder what Joaquina is doing."

"I feel an urge to be exotic."

"You, Esther?"

"Why not? Are you surprised?"

"No, darling, you'd be phenomenal: red panties, with a ruffled tail. You could shake it beautifully."

They all laughed again.

"Silly."

"The worst thing would be for you . . ."

"The bottle's still almost full."

"I wonder what Eusebio is doing?"

"Oh! These mothers."

"Well, he's so adorable."

"If *you* didn't say so . . ."

"I say so, too."

"Naturally, both of you. And in a little while Esther and I will have a house full of children and we'll tell you about everything they do. They'll be marvelous, won't they?"

"Like you."

Like me, thought Hugo, and suddenly the church and the trees acquired the same rhythm as the piece the marimba was playing, and laughter sounded, an automobile tire screeched, and a legless beggar approached on a small platform with skate wheels. The man asked for help and Hugo gave him a five peso bill, and the vendor of cheap Spanish jewelry came over: "From Toledo, genuine Toledo."

Hugo picked up a small knife, a letter opener.

"Don't, Hugo. You are hurting me!"

"Stick her with something else, buddy," shouted a passerby.

Hugo flared up and looked around for the owner of the voice, but now the people in front of him were a fat gentleman with his wife and behind him were some women.

"Come on, drink up! Don't buy that thing!"

"And if I want to?"

"Buy it!"

"How much?"

"I hope he's not too much trouble."

"Don't worry about it. He's a charming little boy. What did you say?"

"A toast, another toast, please!"

They boarded the ship, pretending to be with the woman in front of them, who was loaded down with parrots in cages.

"We're going to say goodbye to my great-aunt," Hugo explained, although there was really no need to do it because a lot of people were coming aboard and nobody was asking anything. "She's a maniac," Hugo continued, "who thinks that since she can't take us with her in person, she has to carry symbols that represent us. I'm that parrot, the one with the blue tail."

"Delightful," Lorenza exclaimed, holding back her laughter as they reached the deck.

"It's not just the way I lie. It's my Asturian charm."

"From Villaviciosa," Lorenza said.

"If you make too much noise they'll chase us off. Now here we are. Let's go inside. What we need is some Spanish brandy."

"Don't you think that's too much for one day?"

"But, my adorable Lorenza, there's still a lot of day left. Lots of hours, lots of drinks. Don't tell me you're ready to go back to the cold. Are you?"

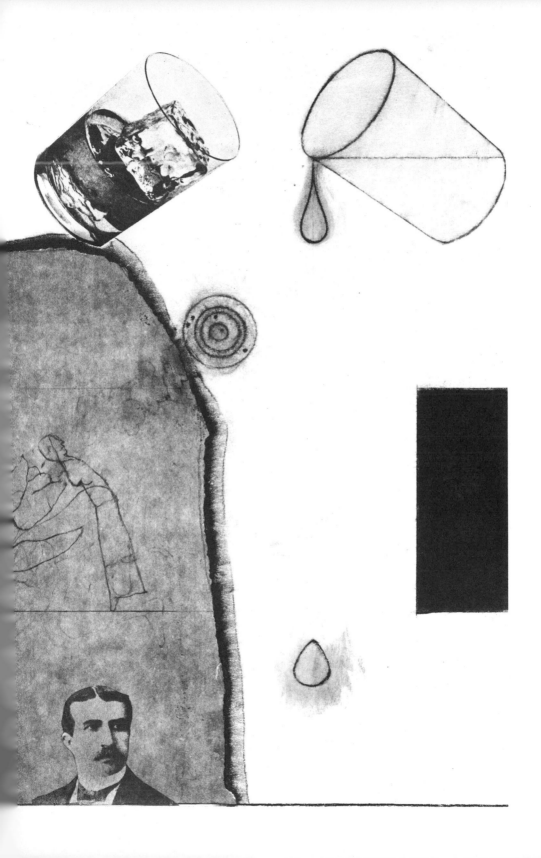

"The aunt who was going in front of us has disappeared. Whom do we belong to now?"

"Now tell them you're a Coviella, daughter-in-law of Eusebio Coviella, who came to Mexico on September 12, 1920—almost, almost as ancient as Hernán Cortés. You are, in a manner of speaking, the history of Mexico."

"And you are an idiot. Go on in."

They went into the smoking room and followed the stream of women and men down below to the bar. The place was on the point of bursting. Voices grew louder as if they suddenly were in Madrid in a cafe at midnight.

"No, we don't want sidra. Bring us something more distinguished."

"Don't shout, he already said yes."

"It's the last they'll permit us," the waiter said. "Not another one until we're on the high seas."

"We hope it lasts until then," Gabriel said as he paid the bill.

"Tum te tum te tum te tum! Tum te tum te tum te tum!"

"Your health!"

"Your health and a thousand times over."

The bar was completely full. Spanish families who were there to say goodbye to their relatives. Mexicans who were leaving for the first time. Everyone seemed happy. Esther smiled. The scene was exactly what she had imagined, gaiety, noise. A tear, a kiss from an old lady, the execessively red cheeks of somebody's grandfather. Another family, perhaps newlyweds: her face—innocent, dark, and pretty—looking at a man who resembled Hugo. A little distance away a woman adjusting her false teeth and later her voice. She couldn't hear her but the movement of her lips was funny. Esther looked through a skylight and saw a light trace of cloud. Hugo shook her to get her attention.

"Let's go," he said.

"But we just got here."

"You don't understand." He took her by the elbow, urged her, "Let's go."

"Wait a minute, we still have some brandy left."

"I mean you and me! Let's go—the two of us—go anywhere, for always."

"Hugo, you're squeezing me!"

"Will you?" he begged.

"Will I what?"

"You and me . . ."

"But my darling, what are you saying?"

"You and I could go away. I don't want to go back ever!"

"Hugo, what's the matter with you?"

"Please, don't ask! Don't ask! Pay attention to me! Let's go!"

"But we came with them." She pointed to her brother-in-law and Lorenza. "Where would we meet them later on?"

"Don't complicate things. They don't have anything to do with what I'm talking about. I'm talking about you and me. Come on, let's go!"

"I think Hugo needs to go to the men's room," Lorenza said.

"It's over there." Gabriel pointed.

Esther looked at Lorenza gratefully. Hugo hesitated a few seconds and stood up. He walked between the filled tables, staggering slightly.

"Go with him, please," Esther begged.

Gabriel followed him.

"The damned! The blind! The destitute! This ill-willed land so bright and so cruel! This world of metallic folly. This hour that disowns you all. Disowns you! Disowns you!"

A policeman arrested a woman a few feet from them and Lorenza felt relieved. She didn't like these scenes, this contact with weakness and misery. She knew she was deceiving herself, but still she preferred that nothing unexpected should ever happen in her presence, nothing that would involve her in an act that she had not anticipated (avoided). She had come to have a good time and she was not going to be deterred, so she was glad that the policeman took the woman by the arm and made her go with him. She stopped looking at her so she would not have to think about unpleasant things. Her chin trembled and she felt that the skin was tense. It's because I've been drinking, she said to herself. I've never drunk like this before. She was almost at the point of feeling guilty when she heard the marimba again not far from their table. Its rhythm infected the *Portales'* customers and suddenly everyone was submerged in the music, saved . . . indifferent, wise, drunk.

The night appeared before her in its full imagery. The stars over the church, the sky like a picture postcard showing the Magi looking at the star—blue, a limpid blue bordered by stars, an incongruous accompaniment to the rhythm of the danzón. Veracruz is vulgar, detestable.

She hated the tendency toward boldness and promiscuity that was characteristic of the place. She, Lorenza Landero, had no validity (her name) in this place. She opened her eyes, drew on her cigarette, saw people passing in front of her—the whole world. For the first time in her life she knew she was drunk and she didn't care. She didn't care about anything or anybody. Gabriel seemed to be distant, immensely distant in his sobriety, apart from her, from her disgust, from her need to vomit. The night scene—dirty, horribly dirty—danced before her eyes, became mixed with the faces—closer and closer—of Hugo and Esther, who were almost kissing. Imperceptibly she made a signal to Gabriel, a slight movement of her fingers in a strange request for help. It was the first time he had ever seen this signal and still he understood it immediately and got up and went with her as if it were all about something entirely different, as if she were not going to vomit. And the floor—black, white mosaics, black, white, black—moved rapidly as she stared at it, until finally she bumped against the door. She went in. She was a lady. I promised it, I said I would do it, that today I would get drunk. The lights made circles in front of her, making her dizzy, so she had to hold on to the edge of the stool. Disgust and laughter blended together as she thought that it was not she, that nobody knew that she . . . that there is no such thing as cold, I am not cold. And when she thought about it, her nausea chilled her and she vomited until she was weak and trembling.

She cared nothing at all about what was happening there, in that revolting little toilet. She cared only that Gabriel was out-

side waiting for her and that she adored Gabriel and that . . .
She vomited again. It just could not be that she, Lorenza
Landero . . . Her father, Don Ernesto, yes. And why my father?
Poor victim of tuberculosis! Hereditary! Surely hereditary! And
then I, his only daughter, full of crazy ideas. Filled with an un-
reasonable desire to perpetuate the line. For what? What has
my Eusebio to do with this . . . with all this? And as she thought
these things, she again saw the plaza, now full of couples. It
was late and they should start back very soon.

"And you'll be sorry," Hugo said to Esther.

"What?" Lorenza asked.

Esther responded by shaking her head, indicating that Hugo
had not said anything important.

The air was dense, motionless, like the heat of an electric
oven over them. A waiter was cleaning the table next to theirs.
Esther remembered that they had not eaten, that they had been
drinking the whole afternoon and into the night.

The marimbas resumed the noisy attack on their ears, but
now the music was sad and tiring.

She rested her elbows on the table, watched Lorenza smoke,
looked at Gabriel's pale face, his eyes watching the passersby,
the cars . . . Hugo, depressed, staring vacantly . . .

"Yes," she said, whispering the words close to his ear, "let's
go away. Hugo, do you hear me? I'm saying yes, I agree with
you. We'll never come back. Hugo . . ."

"No! It's too late!"

"Why are you shouting?"

"Forget it. It was just a game and now it's over."

"Here's to us!"

"Let's go . . ."

chapter 14

"The flower of the dead is yellow and in November the fields are covered with yellow."

"A flower for each one who has died."

"You two are nuts, one because he's old and the other because he's loaded down with kids," Lucio said.

"Flowers are money for you," Francisco replied. "Because of them you can support María better."

"It's better to have flowers than to have kids like a rabbit."

"Because you can't have any."

They finished putting up the cows and went to the entrance of Liborio's house. There they sat down under the shed roof with their backs against the wall and looked at the cold afternoon, waiting for Liborio's wife to come out to offer them a little coffee or liquor.

They heard the shots again.

"You want to go?"

"It's cold. They'll be back before long."

"You're getting old, Alejandro."

They could see how the fog came down and touched the grass. In the background the black skeletons of apple trees were transformed into stumps by the fog. Far away they heard a song.

"Cristóbal must be sleeping off his hangover," Francisco said. "The stuff went to his head today."

"Hangover nothing, he's been cleaning the pigsties."

"The old man always defends him."

The shots sounded again and a gust of wind brought the sound of a voice: "I win."

"Of course Hugo won."

"Señor Gabriel won it last time."

"Yes, but it was nothing but luck, because Hugo's a better shot."

"I hope the loser pays off with a bottle. It's cold enough."

"Sometimes Señor Hugo seems to be nervous."

"But he takes a drink and then he's over it."

"He probably wishes he had a child," Francisco said. "His wife isn't pregnant yet."

"This guy thinks everybody wants children," Lucio exclaimed, laughing. "High class people don't spend all that time having children. Look at Señor Gabriel, one and that's it."

"If I had their money . . ."

Liborio's wife stuck her head out the door and smiled.

"Just a minute . . ."

After standing motionless for a long time, Esther took a step backward, as if she had been on the point of falling in an abyss. She heard clearly the dropping of spring water, heard the silence between drops, sensed—discovered—the immensity of the mist. A sea of fog, that is exactly what it was like, a sea of fog, a monstrous, limitless landscape. It is wonderful . . . it is my house . . . my . . . In a disordered way, their room (hers and Hugo's) was mixed up with this undetermined space. For years I wanted a home, I couldn't have stayed there any longer, enduring the horrible four walls of my hotel room. It's not that I cared so much whether Mamá got married or not. She was young, she should have done it. But there I was, the prisoner of an infinite number of inhibitions and rules that my mother showed me were invalid. I could have left at any time without hurting anyone, but I stayed there waiting for you. I also, like Lorenza, "romantically" waited for you always. She thought of herself living hour after hour, all of them the same. Day after day of heat and loneliness. She remembered looking from her window, spying on the happiness and joy of the innumerable men and women who came and went day in and day out, filling the Nueva Posada de la Suerte—her home . . . And the heat deadening her senses, dehydrating her body, filling her with yearning—and she abandoned in loneliness. Her nights were short, sweaty, exhausting. She had to go downstairs (she used to wake up before anybody else) to swim in the pool when the water was cold and she could feel it like a whip; and she would begin to swim fast, fast, fast, to be warm again. One day, after one of these sessions, when she reached the side of the pool she found his hand. He was waiting for her, smiling the most charming smile she had ever seen. He didn't seem real. He simply was not real. She allowed him to help her, to seat her at the edge of the pool (without a word, with smiles saying everything), and she also let him begin to undress in front of her and she looked at him, charmed. He started taking off his clothes—first his shoes, socks, shirt—and when he let his pants drop, he burst out laughing. "You thought I wasn't wearing trunks." He dived into the pool in his bathing suit. She stopped seeing him (the morning light was blinding) and suddenly she felt that something—someone—was pulling her by the leg into the water. His name was Hugo and she became his sweetheart, and his wife.

The fog, the caress of fog that is warm to one who loves it, came toward her like a thousand kisses from Hugo. She did not want to stop living here; it was her home. The sought-for, imagined dream of one day having a home somewhere. If we were to have a child. If I gave you a child, you would not think of leaving here. They had not talked about it again, but she was certain that in his supplication there had been a real desire to leave, a vehement need not understood by her at the moment when it was expressed.

She felt the cold. The mist totally covered El Bordo. She started walking. When she got in the car the warmth felt good. She turned on the headlights and went very slowly along the narrow road, afraid she might have an accident. On the way the mist became lighter, and when she arrived, the afternoon light still illuminated the Coviella house. She put the car in the garage and saw Hugo going up the hill on the way to Alejandro's house. She thought about calling him but decided she wouldn't. Then she smiled and began to run after him, trying not to make any noise.

Halfway up the hill she met Burgos.

"Come on," she whispered, "let's surprise your master."

The dog kept on wagging his tail.

Humid earth, mossy silence. In the shadows the house loomed like its own ghost. Cautiously she went up to the door and heard steps inside. Then she hit the door hard and opened it abruptly, trying to frighten him.

She went in.

"Darling." Walking almost blindly, she suddenly felt afraid.

Hugo was not there.

"It's me, señora," said Cristóbal behind her.

She was so surprised she couldn't say a word. She tried to smile, to make an excuse, to say something that would take away her fear and change the scene into something trivial. Cristóbal was staring at her uneasily, and suddenly he closed the door and leaned his body against it. Esther realized that he was drunk. But there was no threat in his eyes or in his expression; there was only an infinite supplication, an infinite love, an absurd love that yearned to be shared. Still looking at him she shook her head weakly, negatively, incapable of saying anything. Only Hugo had seen her this way. Then she recovered her strength.

"Open the door, Cristóbal."

Burgos was outside scratching on the wood and whining gently.

Instead of opening the door, Cristóbal took a step toward her, trying to smile. Esther, feeling a wave of disgust, stepped back.

"Your husband isn't here. They all went to the stables. You're alone with me." He was advancing slowly. "I have loved you since you cured my finger. I love you. I love you."

He put out his hand to caress her.

"Indian scum!" Esther screamed.

Cristóbal never actually touched her. He let his hand drop.

"Pardon me." He opened the door and started running toward the woods.

Esther saw Burgos come in wagging his tail happily and she embraced him, crying, filled with fear, and at the same time filled with gratitude. Then suddenly she felt infinitely empty, deserted, drowned in solitude.

"Come," she said to the dog, and fled to the house.

"When night falls one believes in ghosts," Doña Teresa said as she stood by the living room window contemplating the strange movement of the fog. The wind was twisting the shrubs and it seemed that hundreds of ghosts were dancing in a rite of welcome to the night. She thought that if she looked long enough a phantom would appear . . . the ghost of someone . . . of my Eusebio . . . Eusebio died on an afternoon like this and he will come back one of these nights. Suddenly the shrubs disappeared and the edge of the garden became vague.

She continued: "I feel as if something out there is going to take form and come inside with us."

"Don't talk to Eusebio about ghosts, because they'll come. He'll see them."

"Eusebio? What Eusebio?"

"My son, naturally."

"Of course, I forgot. Sometimes I forget things. Everything . . ."

"Except praying."

"If I should forget that, my child, I would go crazy."

Esther came in, pale and trembling.

"Haven't they come back yet?" she asked, going over to the fireplace followed by Burgos.

"No. Where have you been?"

"I went to El Bordo . . . I took a walk."

The logs crackled, giving off security and warmth.

"Why are you sitting in the dark?"

"We're invoking ghosts. What's wrong with you? You look like a corpse. Who frightened you? You need a cognac to get your color back," Lorenza said, glancing at Joaquina in expectation of a reprimand.

But it never came.

Joaquina said wearily, "Give me one too."

Lola had been surrounded by daisies, her skin almost as white as the flowers themselves. For the first time exact and definitive, in the dark coldness of the room, illuminated by her incongruous smile. It was a smile that died within her, that could not infect others or turn into the laughter that had made her charming. Irresponsible Lola, associated in her memory with the intense red of her clothing and her lips, received her forlornly decorated with daisies, covered with a white blanket—mistress of a profound silence that now affected others the way her laughter used to. "Do you remember, Lola?" And Lola's smile assented, remembered, while a nun explained everything to Joaquina. All about the sickness, the medicine, what the doctor had thought. And Joaquina asked her, "Why didn't you think of me before, Lola? Why not before?" And suddenly Joaquina began to cry there in front of Lola's smile, just as she had cried more than thirty years before. "Do you remember, Lola? Do you remember? I also cried that night on the ship when I confessed to you that I didn't love Luis Larragoitia. How you laughed at me!"

"Joaquina!" Lorenza exclaimed, interrupting her memories. "There's something that we haven't told you and I think it's better for you to know it once and for all. Yesterday we went to Veracruz for the day and had a wonderful time."

"I'm glad," Joaquina answered.

"What did you say?" Lorenza asked, surprised.

"What did you say?" Esther repeated.

"That she's glad! She said she's glad," Doña Teresa explained as Joaquina left, sobbing, and went to her bedroom.

"But what's wrong?"

"Her friend Lola is dead. She was dead when Joaquina got there. She had just died."

"But it's absurd for her to cry. I never heard her mention such a friend."

"Oh, yes, dear, she was always talking about Lola Bárcena.

She loved her a great deal. They were friends for years. She hasn't said so much about her recently, but she used to talk about her all the time. They adored each other. That's why she's crying."

"Well, she really must have loved her a lot. Did you notice? She didn't even get mad about the trip."

"But my dear children, why should she object? Did I say anything about it? And I had reason to. Leaving me on the anniversary of my husband's death . . . But I didn't say anything. No, you're young, you must suffer and have your own troubles. I didn't say a thing to you. I didn't get mad. Even though you left me here with nobody but poor Rita, who couldn't go to see her sister because she didn't want to leave me alone. Poor Joaquina! She loved Lola so much. She was pretty, very pretty and flighty. One of those women who people say are bad. Because she never married, because she went here and there thinking that her beauty would last forever. Poor woman! I've already said a prayer for her. Tomorrow my Mass will be for her. Joaquina loved her so. She saw that they gave her a good funeral."

"Eusebio didn't say anything," Lorenza commented.

"The child didn't know anything about it. Why should he? The nuns entertained him while Joaquina took care of all the details, and early today she buried her."

The clock struck seven. The room was lighted only by the fire.

"What a quiet household!" Gabriel exclaimed, and turned on the light. The three women blinked.

"Your aunt got back an hour ago," Lorenza said.

Hugo kissed Esther and asked, "Does she already know about it?"

"I just told her about it. She didn't say a thing."

"Because she's very sad, my son. Her friend Lola died early yesterday morning."

"Where is Eusebio?" Gabriel asked.

"He went to town with Rita."

Gabriel kissed Lorenza and then his mother. Doña Teresa

was murmuring something, praying, remembering, no one knew what. Gabriel sat down near the fireplace and looked at her over by the door with her rosary in her hands. In a way he wished that his mother had died years ago so he might keep only the memory of the happy mother she used to be. A woman who was nothing at all like the one he saw now: this tiny, nervous, vague woman dressed in black and talking with dead people—a woman living in another world. This woman, an infinitely good woman, who cannot understand anything that goes on about her or comprehend the problems of her children. And why? Because of her love for Papá—an excessive, unhealthy love. She idealized Papá. More exactly, she idealized Papá's eyes. Now she was an inexperienced dreamer of a girl (undoubtedly the girl that she had been before she was married), as if her husband's death had made her forget the years of her marriage and the experience became something completely unknown and foreign to her. Mamá once had known how to say, "This is good. This is bad. Don't do it, Gabriel. No, Hugo, pay attention." Suddenly she was saying nothing but prayers. Poor Mamá! She loved him so much . . . He thought about his father. About handsome old (that's the way he remembered him) Eusebio Coviella. Yes, he loved him, he remembered him and associated him with the constant atmosphere of happiness that overwhelmed everything else, nothing but happiness. That's why Don Eusebio could not understand, did not want to know, that he had problems. "Look, son, if you don't want to study, don't study. If you don't want to be a doctor or a lawyer—all right, don't be one." He never explained anything or gave him advice, never let him say why he didn't want to study. "If what you want to do is good, it will be good for you." A beautiful formula. He smiled. Then he reproached himself for smiling. No, I'm not going to blame him . . .

Doña Teresa began to doze. The cat jumped on her lap, looking for a place to sleep. Burgos looked at him, hesitated a minute, and decided he would rather rub up against Hugo's pant leg. Hugo was looking out at the night. So Joaquina knows it and doesn't care. Okay, so much the better. She really loved

Lola. I remember seeing them together lots of times when I was little. Lola was very pretty and nice . . .

"Pa . . . pa . . . pá . . ." Eusebio sang happily as he ran toward him.

Esther went to the window and leaned her forehead against the glass. The house was hemmed in by darkness.

"You love me?" Hugo asked, kissing her gently.

"Yes." She caressed him, still looking outside. "Hugo, let's go away. Don't move. Don't say anything. I don't want us to be here any longer. Let's go away. I'm afraid. All this makes me afraid."

"Silly, winter is always like this. It seems unreal, eternal. You'll see, next month. It'll be colder and there may even be snow. You'll like it."

"Hugo! Hugo! My darling!"

chapter 15

Only the pines kept their green foliage. The constant howling of an icy wind took charge of the mutilation of the garden and the orchards. The day dawned gray, quietly sad. The lawn, a mirror of ice, acquired the dead color of straw.

"I'm old, surely that's why it is, because I'm old," Alejandro said to himself. He finished tying the bundle of logs and threw it on his shoulder. He couldn't understand. For more than a month he had thought about it and hoped that something would happen. Something that would resolve the misunderstanding. He wished for a letter, a message that would explain what had happened. But no news came. He didn't see him again. He only knew what everyone else said, nothing more. At night he imagined he could hear his footsteps, imagined the knock on the door. He would get up to open it and Cristóbal would be seated by the brazier, explaining why he had run away after stealing two pigs, why he had sold them in the market place in town where everybody could see him. The boy is not bad, he is not a thief. Why did he do it? If he needed a little money, he knew I had some . . . And Alejandro shook his head, still wondering, and walked slowly toward the house.

As if Joaquina could guess that he was thinking about Cristóbal, she asked him:

"You still haven't heard anything from that thief?"

"Nothing, señora, nothing. And I say he isn't a thief."

"Oh, no, he isn't a thief," Joaquina said maliciously. "It's a good thing these rascals are too stupid to steal anything valuable, because once a man decides to steal he's not going to have any scruples that would put a limit on the value of what he takes."

Alejandro put the logs near the fireplace and went out.

"May God pardon him," said Doña Teresa. "He was a good man."

"He *is* a good man," Esther replied emphatically. Then she acted confused, and blushed. "I mean he still hasn't died."

Lorenza came in tying a lilac scarf at her neck.

"I'm ready," she said.

Esther stopped the car by the door to Saturnino Linares' office, which was at one side of the cathedral. Curiously, winter enlivened the city. In the park hundreds of birds were singing under the protection of the pine boughs—a durable refuge, secure, always green, always the nesting place of sparrows and thrushes.

A little boy holding his nurse's hand sang as he passed them:

> Oranges and lemons,
> lemons and limes . . .

Behind them a little girl was jumping along trying not to touch the cracks in the pavement and paying no attention to the servant's "Don't fall down and hurt yourself."

"I'll go visit my aunt," Lorenza said.

"No, no!" Joaquina cried, stopping her. "Wait. We can go together in a few minutes, I would like to pay my respects. Come on."

The three of them entered the small office building and the receptionist got up immediately and admitted them to a waiting room. Furniture upholstered in leather, bronze ashtrays, a heavy gray carpet, a prism lamp, and two Degas reproductions on the wall.

Before they could sit down, Saturnino opened the door to his private office and with a charming smile asked them to come in.

"Right on time, Joaquina. Right on time as usual. It's a pleasure to deal with people like you . . . and your fine nieces-in-law. Señoras, come in, I beg you."

Lorenza looked at her watch. It was almost twelve o'clock. Disgusted with herself for having allowed Joaquina's imposition, she lit a cigarette. She couldn't lose much time because she had a lot of shopping to do. She sat on a sofa beside Esther while Joaquina stood by the desk talking with Saturnino. Mentally she went over the list of things she was supposed to get for Gabriel, for Doña Teresa, for Eusebio . . . and for herself. Suddenly she noticed that Saturnino was talking to her.

"Excuse me, I didn't hear you."

"I was saying that it was a pity about your house. When I tried to buy it, it was too late."

"You were going to buy it?" Lorenza asked sharply.

"Of course, if Doña Joaquina had agreed, the day I offered it to her we could have gotten it for two hundred thousand. But when she told me to buy it, it was no longer possible, in spite of the fact that I offered the new owner a hundred thousand more. A Turk bought it. But he wouldn't accept the offer. He thinks his movie theater is an excellent business venture. I said to Doña Joaquina, 'I'll do the best I can, but I think it's wasted effort.' And so it was."

"Lorenza didn't know anything about it," Joaquina explained. "It was going to be a surprise."

The two women looked at each other a few seconds, and then Joaquina looked away.

"I am very grateful to you . . ." Lorenza said.

"It was a pity, a real pity. The floor in your house was a marvel, and they destroyed it, broke it to bits. They're people who don't understand these things. Well . . . Señora Esther is first. Come over here, please."

"Me?" she asked.

"It's another surprise," Joaquina said, feeling uncomfortable. "A gift for you and Hugo. The Las Vigas house is for the two of you. But the deed is in your name."

"But I . . . Doña Joaquina . . . You see . . . You overwhelm me. Hugo knows about it, doesn't he?"

"No."

"He'll go out of his mind. He loves the place so much . . ."

She went over to Joaquina and kissed her. Joaquina answered with a gentle caress.

"And for you, for you and Gabriel," her voice was stiff, uncertain, "I bought you an excellent corner. You can build a fine house near Los Berros, or a hotel, or an apartment building. Whatever you like. I know you prefer the city, that someday . . ." Lorenza interrupted her with a kiss and an embrace.

Esther accelerated as they left the town of La Joya. She wanted to get home as soon as possible to tell Hugo the news. Lorenza watched the rapid passage of the pine trees that grew out of the lava and became steadily higher and weaker.

"Why did you do it, Joaquina?" she asked, still watching the trees.

There was a long silence. Then she answered hoarsely, "How do I know? Yes, I do know. But I tried to remedy it."

"No, no," Lorenza interrupted. "I don't mean that. I mean this house. Why are you giving it to us?"

Another silence. Finally, with no emotion, "Because it's Christmas."

chapter 16

It rained every day for more than two weeks. The tree trunks were covered with moss and the road with mud. It was very cold. Every morning the fields were carpeted with ice. Joaquina looked at the fine rain that fell so slowly it seemed to be suspended on the air. She remembered winter in the mountains of Asturias, a walk to Villaverde to visit a relative. She remembered the interminable and happy ascent of the mountain while snow fell slowly, very slowly, like this winter rain that year after year obliged them to stay shut up in the house. They spent almost all their time in the living room, repeatedly stepping over the make-believe trains that Eusebio made with the fireplace logs. Burgos had to move constantly because the boy's railroad invariably passed right through the center of the place where the dog was sleeping. But Burgos never got angry. He patiently accepted his displacement and licked his master's face.

"Happiness is something that belongs to children and dogs," Hugo said.

"Aren't you happy?"

"If I could only leave here this minute, if I could only go somewhere, anywhere."

"Not me," Esther answered as she finished threading her needle. Doña Teresa was teaching her to embroider and she was learning rapidly. "I don't want to go anywhere. I'm content here in spite of the cold."

She didn't dare say "I'm happy" for fear that if she put her thought into words her happiness might seem too easy or false. She preferred not to think, as if the thought itself might betray her or make her become the agent that would destroy her own happiness. Her fingers trembled as she held her needlework and her little finger caressed the red of some cherries that she had just embroidered. She wanted Hugo or Eusebio to start laughing, she wished that something funny would happen, something that would change the menacing pattern that caused her anxiety . . . Then like someone who looks for the proof of a fact—although she was only pursuing a hope—her eyes fell upon the thick wall through which an archway led to Joaquina's bedroom and office. The solidness of the stone pleased her, as if it were a kind of sign favorable to her longing. Then tranquilly, sure that no clever enemy could disrupt the order of her feelings, she looked over the rest of the room. The clock with its large mahogany case, its pendulum and counterweight recently polished by Gabriel; the rough wall, inviting, with a portrait of young Luis Larragoitia placed precisely in the center, according to an aesthetic canon based on exactness; the window with its steamed-over panes, the passage of some recent drops held up by the intense cold . . . She felt that if she stood up she could see the arroyo, which always made her feel calm. The wall continued its rusticity, broken—or corroborated —by another portrait. Don Eusebio Coviella. He was also young, also perfectly placed in the center, his eyes condemned to look at a gray wall with no decoration, because surely his range of vision did not include the enormous fireplace, where he might have been provided some diversion by the silver sugar bowl exquisitely decorated with vague faces of cherubs and virgins, or by the portraits of his grandson, or of his sons . . . But Esther hardly noticed all these different things, because it all came together for her in a single and stable feeling of warmth and company whose center was the crackling of the logs, the welcome yellow-blue-orange color. And then nearer her, bathed by the reflections from the fireplace, her husband's trousers, drill cloth covering the hair on those legs that knew how to entwine themselves so readily and gently with her own.

And Esther thought that this is how it was yesterday and the day before and for many days, and she hoped that it would never change. She asked only this—the worshipful contemplation of a happiness that she could not express in words.

The peacefulness of being together, of having a place to go to rest, a place to talk, to feel a part of a family, a place . . .

"Of course you're talking about wanting to go away in order to tell me that you don't care about the house," Joaquina said, "and since you don't care about it you don't have to be grateful for the gift. Right? Well, keep the comments to yourself! And keep your gratitude to yourself, if you've ever had any. I don't need it."

"Yes, it does matter to him, Doña Joaquina," Esther interrupted. "You know he's . . ."

"Don't tell me what he's like, I know him better than you do."

"Yes," Hugo shouted, "I have a tail and horns, and I breath fire. And nobody asked you for your lousy house. The only reason you gave it to us was so you could feel good and generous. But you're not fooling anybody and you're not as magnanimous as you pretend you are. My father worked for you plenty without getting anything for it, and now I'm knocking myself out."

"You and your father. A fine pair of loafers."

Esther looked at her instruction book: "the stems colored, with medium green and soft green, edges brown, as in illustration number nine." It would pass soon, she thought, it is better not to worry about them, it is better not to listen to them.

"Which green do you think would be better for the stem?" she asked Doña Teresa, who came in at that moment.

"Have you finished the cherries already? Look how pretty they are!"

She didn't listen to her mother-in-law either. She saw Eusebio over by the fire, kneeling on a lambskin rug—withdrawn and silent—building a tower on Burgos' back. Perhaps he too had learned not to listen. They were all in on the secret; they understood this game that nullified them and that had made Lorenza exclaim with desperation a few nights before, "At times I have the feeling Joaquina and Hugo are the only ones who exist. What about us?"

"It's true," Esther murmured. They were in the dining room after the meal had been ended by a heated discussion. The two women and Gabriel sat before their empty cups, playing with crumbs of bread. Suddenly the embarrassing silence was broken by the laughter (it didn't seem possible) of Joaquina and Hugo, who were happily enjoying something very funny. Esther continued, "They seem . . . they're so sure of themselves, so solid."

"Listen to them. They live in a world of their own and act as if everything else belonged to them too. And what about us? What are we?"

"Ghosts," Gabriel answered, raising his shoulders and eyebrows at the same time. "But since they don't believe in ghosts they can go to the devil as far as we're concerned."

A few seconds later Hugo came in smiling, with Eusebio in his arms.

"Shall we play lotto?" he asked.

It was as if nothing had happened. That night they played longer than usual.

Esther burst out laughing and Eusebio's tower fell to the floor.

"I can't do it," he said. "Will you play with me?"

She put her needlework aside and knelt on the rug so the two of them could start rebuilding the tower on the bare floor. A nearby log smelled intensely of resin. The scent of the perfume pleased her. She remembered the intense perfumes of Cuernavaca and thought about her mother. About her incongruously happy marriage. Because she (her mother) was happy too in her hotel with her Hans Meyer, and what was most absurd of all, Hans also lived happily. So happiness was, is, an inconsistent and foolish picture to the eyes of an outside observer. She must never be the observer of her own happiness. What can one possess without the risk of loss or scorn? This: some alphabet blocks, the satisfaction of building towers that fall but can be rebuilt over and over again until you get tired of it, the warmth and gentleness of the logs in the fireplace, and especially living together with a group of antagonistic beings. Yes, but by the side of that common denominator of antagonism there also existed a solid relationship whose durability one could sense. At least she had the security of living facts, things, and direct contact. This last thought went through her mind as she felt her husband's hands—rough, calloused, and warm—caressing her. Hugo leaned over and bit her hair, laughing.

"Little girl, would my sweetie like to play with her dolls?"

Esther leaned her head back against his legs and caressed his hands, which were on her cheeks.

"I love you as much as I love Burgos," Hugo said, biting her hair again.

"Are you sure?" she asked, looking at the fire and feeling indestructibly happy.

"The car!" Eusebio shouted, getting up rapidly.

Lorenza and Gabriel brought a gust of icy wind in with them. Their faces were red from the cold. She took a few rapid steps forward as she took off her wool muffler and top coat. She had had her hair cut in the city and it fell over her forehead with a studied carelessness in a presumably cosmopolitan style. Her mannequin-like appearance was accentuated as she stood beside the solid simplicity of her husband.

"We went by to pick up the mail in town," Lorenza said.

They saw the letters in her hand. Esther thought that one was from her mother—she saw the envelope with advertising on it. Joaquina took her letters, looked at the names of the senders, and didn't bother to open them. She preferred to look at Lorenza's new hairdo.

"Aunt Amelia sends regards to everybody," Lorenza said, reading the postcard again. "She says she's tired of looking at snow."

"Is she well?" Doña Teresa asked.

But her question really didn't anticipate an answer, and Doña Teresa stared absent-mindedly at the flames while Esther looked at a tardy offer from a publishing house advertising their latest novels for Christmas gifts. Gabriel served himself a large cognac and Hugo took advantage of the opportunity to do the same. Lorenza remembered the last thing her Aunt Amelia had said before leaving for New York: "I don't even know any more why I'm going to take this trip. At first I told myself that I wanted to get to know the last place your Aunt Lorenza visited before her death. But I think that was only a pretext, because in reality I hardly remember my sister. Anyway . . . I already have my ticket." And unenthusiastically she boarded the airplane. Then the postcards had come. Lorenza could not understand what her Aunt might find there that would be interesting or diverting, since she was alone and unable to speak English and at an age when she could hardly expect adventures or romance.

"When is it going to snow, Mamá?" Eusebio asked.

"Tomorrow," she answered.

"Or day after tomorrow," Gabriel said.

"Snow?" Doña Teresa asked.

She tried to imagine Doña Amelia Landero in snow, a lot of snow. She saw her get out of an automobile wearing a long coat with a fur collar and going into the French department store. As she passed in front of her she gave a slight nod and a half smile as if she were asking herself, "Who is . . .?" "Who is she?" Eusebio asked her. "Amelita Landero, she belongs to one of the oldest families in the city. But she's been living in Puebla for years. She's pretty, isn't she?" And they continued walking. She was carrying Gabriel, who was two years old. Then many years passed before they saw each other again. Almost thirty years: the wedding of Lorenza and Gabriel. She had become a mature woman, but elegant and vivacious, heiress to a name and to a way of living that she knew how to carry off perfectly—now that she was rich again. She again received Jalapa society with the same prodigality and elegance that had characterized her ancestors. Joaquina had commented: "She is the most discreetly ostentatious woman I have ever known." "I think she is charming"—Doña Teresa expressed her opinion emphatically—"a real Jalapa lady." Basically both of them were well satisfied with the wedding.

"Lorenza has some news," Gabriel said.

They all looked at her.

"I'm going to have a baby. The doctor says in September."

Esther got up quickly and embraced her.

"You see," she whispered, pressing her cheek against Lorenza's, "you also exist."

"What did you say?" Lorenza asked without understanding at first.

"That you also are living, not just the two of them."

Lorenza hugged her tighter.

"Soon, you too. You'll see."

"I want a girl," Gabriel said, satisfied.

"This time it will be a girl," Doña Teresa said. "We will knit her only pink things."

"When is it going to snow?"

"I'll tell you whether it's going to be a boy or a girl when I see the shape of your body," Joaquina said, and she came over to kiss her too. "I remember back in Spain we were always happy when someone was going to be born. And I can't understand why, because there were too many of us already."

"It will be a girl," Doña Teresa said. "It will be a girl."

"You're going to have a little sister, Eusebio."

Lorenza would have liked to be alone with Esther so she could tell her how happy she was. Happier than she had thought she would ever be again. She didn't care about her house. What she cared about was the living being inside her, perhaps even more than the first time (or have I forgotten about when Eusebio was going to be born?). It was like inheriting a fortune unexpectedly, as if somehow she had become a more authentic version of herself, a past full of meaningful events all dependent on one another. She must think about the future again. She accepted the dissolution of her past in exchange for the presence of another being who would place her definitively in this epoch from which she had felt separated. Her mistake was obvious now; Eusebio was already different from her. For him "the Landeros" would at best evoke compassion and at worst a kind of mythomania.

"I feel unscrupulously and stupidly happy," she exclaimed, kissing her son.

"We should drink a toast," Gabriel said.

"There won't be anything very unusual about that," Joaquina said. "But you're right, we should have one."

A few minutes later Esther discovered that Hugo was no longer in the living room. Trying not to attract attention, she went out to the hall and went up the winding staircase.

"Hugo," she whispered. "Why did you run away?"

"Run away?" he answered, without showing any surprise either because of her being there or because of her question. "Are you crazy?"

"Why did you run away?"

"I'm here because I want to be here. Because I want to be alone."

"Because you're envious."

"Be quiet. Go away and stay with the others."

"Hugo, don't talk to me that way."

"What? Are you threatening me?"

"I am asking you . . . Don't create a problem."

"Over what?"

"You know perfectly well. Over Lorenza's being pregnant when I'm not."

"I haven't said . . ."

"Of course you haven't. You haven't dared say anything. But say it, Hugo. It bothers you that I'm not pregnant. Me too, Hugo. But say it! Scold me, if you want too."

"You're crazy. You're exaggerating."

"No, I'm not. Every month you ask me if my period has started. You know the date better than I do. Tell me if it's not true."

"Yes, of course it's true. But I won't ask you any more and I won't say anything about it. I want a son. Is there anything wrong in that?"

"No, my darling. I want one too. But it isn't my fault."

"You mean it's my fault?"

"No, Hugo, no. I don't mean that, and I don't want you to get mad. I'll go see a doctor."

"You don't have to see a doctor."

"But it could be that there's something wrong with me. It could be my fault. I've never blamed you."

"No, but you thought it. You think it, and that's enough. I don't want to talk about it anymore. After all, it would take more than a child to make us happy."

"I don't understand you. What does your happiness depend on? What *is* your happiness? It seems to be so many things and still none of them. How can I know? Only a month ago you were very pleased by the gift of the house."

"The house! Some shit! She didn't fool anybody when she put it in your name."

"I don't understand you," Esther said again, shaking her head and almost weeping.

"Burgos understands me and that's enough."

"It's possible," she whispered, going down the stairs.

She heard the happy voices in the living room and for the first time since she was married she wanted to be with her mother, she wanted to embrace her, even though Doña Esther would not be able to share her troubles or even guess what she needed. She thought about calling her on the telephone. But what good would it do?

chapter 17

A flash of lightning suddenly illuminated the garden.

"It's a perfect night for a murder."

The thunder made Esther jump. She put her hands over her ears and shouted, "Can't you talk about anything else?"

Lorenza lifted her eyebrows and understood her mistake. Before her the night once more became a limitless black pit whose reality existed only in her own thoughts. The dogs began to howl—a pervasive and mournful howl. The storm had caused a breakdown in the electrical installation, and the living room was illuminated only by candles. Another flash of lightning again made the garden blindingly bright, and immediately its corresponding thunder shook the walls. Lorenza noticed that Esther was trembling with fear. On account of the storm, or on account of Hugo? She wondered, and repeated to herself that it was a perfect night for a murder. A few minutes earlier Gabriel had gone to town to look for Hugo, who had disappeared after dinner. She lit a cigarette and her hands trembled. She was nervous, but it had been a long time since storms had made her afraid. Her nervousness now came from boredom, from the long confinement to which all of them had been sentenced by the bad weather—a confinement that was the basic cause of Eusebio's crying, and of the collective irritability that was palpable in the atmosphere, as if it were a clear proof of the deficiency of human relationships—a deficiency that made them feel ashamed and that they sometimes tried to overcome with a weak attempt at humor that was quickly and brusquely over-whelmed by the first trivial disagreement. Lorenza knew she was worse than the rest of them because the nausea of preg-nancy upset her nerves for the first three months . . . She leaned her forehead against the windowpane, drew on her cigarette without enjoying it, and heard the thunder again. What could she do? There were six or seven books in her library that she hadn't read, but she was sick of murder mysteries. If only there would be a little sun tomorrow, if only the day would begin without being covered by fog and cold . . . We could go to Jalapa. But why? Aunt Amelia was still in New York, prolong-ing her useless trip. Or could it be that she was enjoying herself there, alone? Had she been to the Statue of Liberty? Had she visited some museums? Had she bought clothing on Fifth Ave-nue? And what for? What does she do then? Does she shut her-self up in her room or does she stay in the hotel lobby and watch the other tourists? There is something indefinably absurd about the whole affair, something that I'll probably inherit, that I'll repeat when I'm sixty years old, just to perpetuate her memory and influence. And I may even find it natural, sensi-ble . . . No, no! I'll tell her that she's a fool, that her trip to New York seems to me to be snobbish and lamentable. We'll quarrel until I feel fond of her again and she makes me laugh. She'll be delighted when she finds out that I'm going to be a mother again. She'll say, "Another Landero!" It will never occur to her that my children will be, are, Coviellas . . . "Another Landero!" She'll be a little girl and she'll look like her father. We'll name her Laura. And she'll be beautiful in lavender, and when she gets married I'll give her my grandmother's necklace.

"Lorenza, the child has gone to sleep here," Doña Teresa said in a low voice, pointing to the little body curled up on the sofa. "Put him to bed."

"Wait until Gabriel comes back. He won't be long."

"He left more than half an hour ago," Esther said.

"Say a prayer, my child," Doña Teresa said.

Joaquina came in with a candle in her hand.

"Haven't they come back? Why did he go away?" she asked

without addressing anyone in particular. "Why did he go away today?" She looked anxious, deeply concerned. "Today he didn't argue with me. Did he argue with you, Esther?"

"No."

Joaquina put out the candle, left it on the fireplace, sat down in her usual chair, and looked at Esther.

"What is wrong with him? What is he thinking about?" she asked, but Esther only shook her head, saying nothing. Joaquina was hurt by Esther's troubled expression. "Ever since he was a small boy he has made us suffer by running away. Always playing that the wolf was after him. Little by little he has gotten an advantage over us by playing on the fear we feel every time he runs off—and he knows it perfectly well. He takes comfort in our fear, in torturing us. That's the way my father used to be. That's the way he always held us in his grip. I was so afraid of him that every time he yelled at me I would start to tremble and ask myself what I had done bad. What could I have forgotten . . .? And he would burst out laughing when he saw how afraid I was. If we let Hugo follow his instincts, he will be the same way, he will dominate us. First with the fraud of his possible danger, with the anguish of wondering whether something has happened to him. And later on, when he sees he has us in his power, he will be like his grandfather, and that I will not permit. Not as long as I live! You shouldn't have told him that I put the house in your name, because now he thinks he is the master of everything. And he is not going to be, because before I allow that I will burn this house, butcher every animal, and leave them here until they rot."

"He no longer cares about the house," Esther said.

Joaquina hardly heard what Esther said. Immersed in her anger, she saw herself destroying it all, annihilating the livestock against the protest of the astonished workmen. They looked at each other and they looked at her, and Joaquina shouted to impose her will, and blood began to flood from the necks of the beautiful Swiss cattle. The pigsties were also destroyed. We will continue the destruction there and then burn the house—everything together. Bring some gasoline, quick!

The flames of her imagined fire became confused with the flames of the fireplace that Lorenza had just tended. Joaquina's eyes grew wide as she looked at the fire. But I am still rich, she thought, I still have the houses in Jalapa and money in the banks and money on deposit with Saturnino—a lot of money when I am dead, money for my heirs, for them. Nothing for the ones over there.

Over there . . . She was never able to remember Villaviciosa without bitterness, without feeling resentment and recalling deprivations that were still as bitter as ever. Sure they would like to have this house, and they would crawl on their bellies before me to get it. "They," who occasionally sent a newspaper from Gijón, a magazine from Oviedo, pages where they talked about "Asturias in Mexico" and for which they requested a photograph of her that would be the illustration for an article that might be headlined "Woman from Asturias is great success." Gerardo, Joaquina's oldest brother, submitted a story for her approval: "Joaquina Coviella, widow of Larragoitia, an intelligent, handsome woman, who was able to rise above the terrible loss of her beloved husband and is now one of the richest . . . most charitable . . . full of optimism . . . pride of Villaviciosa and of all Asturias . . . We look forward with open arms to her return . . . to this corner of the world that she has never forgotten." She wrote to Gerardo asking him to stop talking foolishness, told him that this was not the way to persuade her to come and even less to exploit her, that once more she would tell him that she didn't want to see them nor did she have any reason to help them. "And as for that nephew who is so bright and who loves and admires me so much, let him study to be a priest and don't count on me to bring him to America." Her sisters also—Conchita, Mercedes, Carmen—used to write letters and they also had a son or a grandson, "little Johnny who loves you even though he doesn't know you and always mentions you in his prayers." Sometimes, but very rarely, she sent them money, clothing, and a few trifles. Soon after Luis's death she had tried to overwhelm them with gifts. But Lola Bárcena had warned her, "Keep this up and they'll ask you for more and more. Then they'll get tired of the gifts and will want to immigrate, and in five years you will have them here living at your expense, thinking that you are a witch because you didn't give them everything they want. And what bothers me is that I won't be able to visit you any more because they must be the incarnation of boredom and nuisance." Lola Bárcena . . . Life was a bundle of loose threads, a finding and losing of people, a wanting of things that make no sense once you have them, a blind building and destroying of little things, trying to fill a vacuum that is too narrow to contain anything. And in the final analysis, what is one after? "You manage to live," she thought weakly, "as if your mouth were full of spider's webs whose threads you don't want to break by breathing. Is this really living?" she asked herself, looking about the room, sensing the tension of waiting in the guarded gestures of Esther, in the little shocks that she felt every time the lightning flashed, in her sister-in-law's muttering of half-spoken prayers, in the tapping of Lorenza's long fingernails on the windowpanes. Not living like this! No! But to really live! Yes! For someone like Lola Bárcena. For someone like Hugo. To live loving. Living in order to share. And with these two she could no longer share any-thing . . .

"Sometimes I think I may go to Spain," she exclaimed.

"To Spain?" asked Doña Teresa, surprised. "What on earth for?"

"For no reason . . ."

chapter 18

And so it was that spring covered the land and a wave of fertility brought life back to the trees; the brilliant white of the plum and pear blossoms looked like the snow that Eusebio had waited for. And it was the sun—the sun was shining—that turned the apple blossoms red with color and light, as if the land, in giving birth, had sent its blood upward into the light to be the token of the future apple. The trunks of the fruit trees lost their dark, winter bitterness and became once more the living conduit of a secure and complete life. The sky above— an ingenuous and shy blue—looked as tranquil as the surface of a lake. At five in the morning the sound of the village church bells joined the awakening countryside and vibrated in the orange-red of the horizon that stood still for a brief moment on the edge of the hills, cutting away the dry green of old pine trees and betraying their innumerable opaque fruits. Life flowed on like eternal waves in eternal rhythm. Even in the roads— where animals and automobiles passed constantly—sprigs came up like uninvited guests who have crashed the party.

"You'd think the whole world had been watered with cognac," Hugo said, "because so much joy could only come from alcohol."

Esther's laughter, rather than a reply to what her husband was saying, was a reaction to Eusebio's fall, and more than to the fall itself, to the expression of the child as he immediately looked up to see if he would be reprimanded for his clumsiness and for having gotten mud on his white silk shirt, and wondering if he would be able to clean it and avoid being quarreled with when he got back home. Before being permitted to go with his aunt and uncle to El Bordo, he had been warned: "If you get dirty, Aunt Amelia is not going to give you the presents she brought you." And they had talked so much about those gifts that Aunt Amelia was going to bring him when she came back. But now Aunt Esther, still laughing, was cleaning his shirt. Esther was thinking that she would never be strict with her children, because although she had been amused by Eusebio's expression, she was also aware of the childish fear, almost an animal fear, of being punished for transgressing one of the innumerable rules that circumscribe the life of a child. She would not do it, she would simply accept these little accidents and would never be both cause and judge of inevitable childhood tragedies that do not fit any frame of reference. She would laugh with her Hugo when he did these things. Her little Hugo, just like his father and still a good deal like her, or with her little . . . not Esther. If I have a little girl I will name her something else.

"Come, run with me, give me your hand," Eusebio asked.

As she gave it to him, she asked herself, "Is it bad for me to run?" and she answered the question by laughing at her excessive concern. Now that the news was corroborated, she was no longer afraid; she felt only an unmeasurable, stupid, sublime joy which was intensified by the fact that it was a secret and even more so by the satisfaction of knowing that this was the day—"Today, Dear God, I will tell him!"—when it would cease being a secret for the family. This was exactly the right place to tell him something so important.

"Here . . . here . . ."

Her words flew through the air, became one with the light, with the shining pines, with the emerald sod beneath their feet, with the wild flowers and the transparency of the air—all of it together the symbol of the harmony and universal happiness in which she was finally taking part. When she was fourteen, Esther asked herself for the first time in her life if she was happy (it was a hot day and she had to spend hour after hour going from one end of the hotel to the other, setting tables, killing flies, serving a cool drink to a guest, quarreling with the servants in her most adult tone—a morning, an interminable day measured in fatigue, sweat, and hundreds of steps) and she knew that she was not, because she was burdened with too many obligations and not enough time to enjoy herself. Her happiness was limited to her mother's occasional caresses when the older Esther chose to pay attention to her daughter rather than to the business affairs of the inn. Once in a while in the evening she would say something nice, would commend Esther for her activity, would tell her that she looked pretty with her apron on. And Esther would gnaw on her words as if the compliment were a bone, would repeat the sentence and discover in it a hidden affection so great that it could be expressed only in this nebulous, sporadic way. But when she was seventeen, just at the time when Hans Meyer appeared, her mother's affection for her became a mere formula or at least was expressed in the same tone that she used to thank a servant for doing a good job. From that time on her own love for her mother became intermittent. Then came her mother's wedding, the transition from a modest inn to a luxury hotel, and the consequent change in clientele, customs, and topics of conversation that relegated her to the shadows and to inactivity. "Don't do that, let the waiters do it." "From now on Hans will take charge of the bank account." "Honey, you don't have to do that." Slowly it reached the point where she no longer had any influence either in the business affairs or in her mother's heart. The hours in Cuernavaca were interminable on account of the heat. At night, before the evening meal, she would stretch out for a while in one of the wicker chairs on the central terrace where the dining room lights were reflected on the floor. She didn't sleep, but closed her eyes, reconstructing the scenes of the meaningless life to which she was confined by a chain of invalid prejudices, concepts, and ambitions. She was disgusted with herself for accepting this emptiness that moved her from this place to that, from one party to another, listening to other people's conversation,

seeing people who did not interest her. She had been attracted
by several of the men whom her mother knew. And she might
even have fallen in love with one of them if they had not all
been so bland, so effeminate, so refined that they were as much
like women as like men. Were there no real men? Leaning back
in the chair on the terrace one night she observed a bee that
was flying furiously around an electric light fixture made in the
form of a large rose, an enormous bud that looked as if it might
be opened up by the electricity. The bee was buzzing fren-
etically about the part that represented the calyx; up higher
the crystal petals began to open but were stopped in their movement by the manufacturer's absurd caprice. Esther knew that
in a few minutes the bee would find the open space in the
petals and fall directly on the bulb, where he would spend his
fury and find his death in fire. That's me, she thought, I am the
bee. She closed her eyes to keep from seeing herself die. Later
on, long after the bee had stopped buzzing, she heard steps and
was informed that her mother and Hans would take a trip to
Germany. Esther immediately began to plan what she would do
while they were away: first of all she was going to show them
that she was in fact useful, that she was entirely capable of
running the hotel all by herself. When they returned from their
trip they would find The Nueva Posada de la Suerte in terrific
shape. They would congratulate her and would realize that they
had shoved her aside unjustly. But all her plans were destroyed
two days later: "No, honey. Rody, Hans's cousin, will take care
of everything. You enjoy yourself." Yes, enjoy herself just like
that bee, drown in the light, immolate herself in the heat. The
trip lasted a year, yet when they came back unannounced, the
reunion was in no way demonstrative or intimate. There was a
friendly chat, some presents, and comments about the photo-
graphs: "A very nice aunt of Hans lives here in Dresden." The
following year she met Hugo, a way to happiness, a road that
was soon darkened by his constant arguments with Joaquina
and also, indeed first of all, by too much cognac, by Hugo's
drinking in an attempt to quench an unquenchable thirst. Yes,
there had been many nights when Hugo, drunk, had gone to

sleep while she was talking with him, halfway through reprimanding him. Then came the horrible January, February, and March with the daily arguments, violent scenes, insults (on the part of both Joaquina and Hugo) that became more and more vicious. Hate was fostered by their obligatory confinement.

Esther almost cried as she rested her hands on the stone fence at the start of the narrow and dangerous horse trail that descended in front of her and now for the first time was bathed in light. She was going to cry for joy on account of the double triumph of having brought her husband to El Bordo. Double because before being told the big news he had happily agreed to come with her just to please her (she considered this an undeniable proof that he still loved her), and also because Hugo had been on the point of getting drunk and had left the liquor in order to come with her so she could tell him, while they were alone, that she was going to be a mother. That would solve all their problems. She had kept the secret two months until there could be no doubt at all. Today was the day. Both she and Lorenza would bear children this year.

"Look, look how pretty," Eusebio shouted, pointing toward the path, where they could see a farm worker ascending, driving his burro. It was a splendid, celestially quiet afternoon.

"Hey," Hugo shouted from the car, "I'll wait for you at the crossing. Catch me!"

"No, Hugo, don't!" she shouted.

But her protest was drowned out when he started the engine. She watched him speed away, and thinking about how much he was enjoying the trick, she herself laughed. After all, it's only a joke. But she would get even. She had a perfect plan. First she would tell him the news that she was two months pregnant and would have a baby in November, and then, when he was enjoying the news to the fullest, she would tell him that it wasn't so, that she had said it only as a joke. What an expression he would have!

"What are you laughing at?" Eusebio asked.

"At your Uncle Hugo, because that rascal would just love to know something that I know."

"What? Tell me!"

"You'll find out, one day you will see. After they bring you your baby brother."

"Mamá says it will be a baby sister."

"And will you love her a lot?"

"Mamá says so."

"And if you have a little cousin . . . a son of mine . . . a little boy who belongs to Uncle Hugo and me? Would you love him too?"

Eusebio examined Esther's face before answering.

He loved her, she was very nice.

"Yes, if he's yours, I will."

"Good. Well, that's the way it's going to be." She bent over, took Eusebio's face between her hands, and confessed to him, smiling, "I'm going to have a baby."

She had said it! It was marvelous to tell someone, because it made it more real, closer to her. It didn't matter that the some-one was Eusebio and that he was incapable of understanding the enormous happiness that the news implied.

"What's his name?" Eusebio asked.

"His name will be Hugo, like your uncle. But don't tell any-body. It's a secret. Come on, let's catch up with him."

"Wait . . . until that man gets up here," he said, pointing to the farm hand.

"No, it would be night. Hurry up!"

She took him by the hand and dragged him away from the fence. The birds in the treetops and on the grass were telling no one knows what stories that afternoon. Esther thought that all nature was talking about pregnancy, child bearing, perpetua-tion—perpetuation not only of the species but of love—and therefore of the stability from which she had felt separated during the long winter that had just passed. In spite of the fact that Hugo represented for her all that was solid and authentic, all that made life worth living . . . in spite of all that, it was by his side that slowly she had come to be uncertain about every-thing. She even came to believe (what a fool I was) that her marriage was a mistake and that she had no reason to be involved in the constant battle that her husband and his aunt carried on. She often felt that she had been the victim of a deception, of a monstrous infamy that had made her marry Hugo. No, dear God! She shouldn't even think that. She shook her head while she walked along the road with Eusebio. I am exaggerating, none of that is right. It's simply that I felt lonely. I thought he didn't love me and he did, he did. Besides, I am not alone, I have him not only in my thoughts and in my heart, but in my body. If I were alone I would be afraid. She laughed. Yes, I would be afraid to walk this road alone. I would think that Hugo had been irresponsible, unreasonably irresponsible, playing a trick on us this way. We have to walk almost a kilometer by ourselves and up here where I used to be so afraid. But now I'm not afraid any more. She squeezed Eusebio's hand and hastened her step. Everything is so peaceful. The sun is shining brightly. It is truly beautiful, but I would rather have taken the walk with him by my side. I wouldn't have been afraid at all . . . I love him so much. He's probably waiting for us, laughing, and he'll make some joke, or make fun of us, especially of me. I can almost hear him: Well, lion-hearted Esther, were you afraid? He's right, I am a coward. The farm hand we saw climbing up is coming toward us now. I hear his steps. He's still a long way away.

"Shall we look for squirrels, Aunt Esther?"

"No, my dear, not now. Hurry up."

"Look! Let's pick those flowers for Mamá."

"Not now, Eusebio, come on. They're a long way away and you might fall into the ravine. Come on now." She took him by the hand again and obliged him to follow her down the road.

"It was thoughtless of Hugo," she said to herself. "He shouldn't have left us alone. That man looks like he's drunk, I think he's singing something. It looks like he fell down."

"Shall we run?" she asked the boy and started running before he could answer.

She still had a good way to go in the silence of thousands of pine trees. The same pine trees that had seemed protective on other occasions when she had walked there, now seemed to be enemies, spies . . . She knew that she shouldn't run so fast, that one of her shoes might slip off at any time and make her fall, and she also knew that such an accident might cause the loss of the child they longed for. Fear constricted her chest. But no, why should I be afraid here? She stopped running and smelled the perfume of the flowers, looked up at the sky and saw the soft blue and the shining light. Millions of luminous points were falling, illuminating, bathing the road with the divine peacefulness of the God that she had learned about in school and from the lips of her mother when Doña Esther was still the woman she had been years ago. This was the God who would give her a child. God is (yes, is) the face of plenitude, the acceptance of happiness and of the infinite.

The scent of resin and forest perfumes filled the air that swept the fine earth from the road; it was a wind that brought with it the echo of distant villages on the sides of the barranca. Those little towns that were so rarely seen, that were guessed rather than seen, clinging to the earth, small houses whose life was made credible to the eye of the distant spectator by a column of smoke that rose up to the heavens. White stains springing up there below—a step away—perhaps a church, perhaps a street, and you could imagine tiny people moving about among the small buildings surrounded by trees, mist, and dreams. One of the towns was called Tatatila, and one day Hugo would go down there and buy beans, and corn, and mushrooms, and some other day he would go down with his son and she would stay home doing needlework or making something in the kitchen for them to eat when they got back . . .

"Why are you crying?" Eusebio asked. "Why don't we go?"

"I'm not crying," she laughed, "I'm not crying, dear."

She kissed him and Eusebio knew that she was crying because her cheek was wet; but he didn't say anything more about it because his mother did exactly the same thing when he asked her why she was crying. She always said she wasn't and then she would kiss him.

Esther noticed that Eusebio was carrying a bunch of the flowers that she had told him not to pick.

"Where did you pick those?" she asked.

"Over there."

He pointed to the most dangerous edge of the barranca. Esther trembled. How could he have done it without her noticing it? How long had they been there? She looked at her watch. It was almost six.

"It's very late. Run!"

But how could Hugo have left them so long? The sun would set in half an hour. It was a lucky thing that La Cruz was so near there, less than a hundred yards away. They made the turn when they came to the curve in the country road and La Cruz appeared, but Hugo wasn't there. Esther went more slowly while she looked over the place—a circular esplanade with a cross in the center which was decorated the third day of each May—trying to locate the car, supposing that Hugo had hidden it behind some pine trees as another one of his typical jokes. She let the child run ahead of her and he shouted happily, "He's not here, Uncle Hugo left us behind," as if it were absolutely the best game of the whole afternoon.

She caught up with him slowly. "But it can't be," she told herself, "he couldn't just leave us here. He knows perfectly well it's dangerous. It's not that the people are bad. Really they aren't bad, but when they get drunk they don't know what they're doing, they lose their senses and women aren't safe around them." She saw Eusebio playing with some stones and was glad that he had not yet learned to be afraid, because she couldn't have stood the fear of someone else. We can keep on going. But where did he go? The road divided at this point, one going toward town while the other led to the farms, to the Coviella house.

The sound of singing—of a drunken singing—came closer. Even before the man appeared she knew that it was the same one they had seen climbing the hill, the one who had followed them, the one who had fallen down. Esther went over to the mountain of stones that Eusebio was building and took one of them. She clutched it in her right hand, hid it behind her back, and returned to the foot of the cross. The man was not yet visible. She looked at her watch. It was almost six o'clock. What an idiot! Her watch had stopped. Then she remembered that she hadn't wound it since the day before. No wonder it was still so light. It's not six o'clock. It's probably about five. I must have been mistaken. Not nearly so much time has passed. Maybe he went to get some cigarettes. Yes, that's probably what it is. It's still very early.

The man came into view and staggered forward without interrupting his song. Esther thought of Cristóbal. It is Cristóbal. No! No, it's not Cristóbal. He was a man about forty years old, dark, dirty, and smiling. His teeth shone like chips of moonlight in his dark face. He stopped, turned around a little, almost with his back to her, and began to urinate. Esther clutched the stone. The man turned his face toward her, still smiling, shook himself, buttoned his trousers, and began to walk toward the cross. The burro followed him slowly, indifferent to the horror of the woman who saw them coming, growing larger, turning into an awful nightmare.

I will kill him, she thought, I will kill him if he comes near me.

"Afternoon, señora. Could you spare a little money?"

"No," she answered. "I don't have any."

"I'm on my way to town," the man said without stopping.

And he continued his journey somewhat insecurely, still smiling. He began singing again as he went away contentedly, taking unusually careful steps.

Esther dropped the stone. "Am I crazy?" she asked herself. "Why did I think he was going to do something to me?" Eusebio was still playing his game, running from one side to the other; the sun was shining, and she heard the engine of an automobile not far away. It's Hugo, she thought, he's coming . . . And then she felt an overwhelming weakness, a desire to fall to the ground and weep. But immediately she reproached herself for giving in like this, and accused herself of being a coward and of exaggerating things. She was not going to meet her husband with a frown. She would smile. And again she felt gay, happy, complete.

"Your uncle is coming," she shouted to Eusebio.

Hugo stopped the car and looked at her smiling.

"Are you mad at me?" he asked.

"No!" she answered, shaking her head, answering his smile and thinking that she would be the one who would make him happy, and that Hugo urgently needed to be happy.

She let him give her a kiss. But it was not the effusive, ardent kiss that she expected. It was a light kiss on her cheek, a kiss with a strong scent of alcohol. She watched him run toward Eusebio, who ran away shouting happily.

Esther shouted: "Hugo, my darling, I have something to tell you."

She smiled, she could yell to him, "I'm going to have a baby." That would stop him in his tracks and he would turn around to her with his eyes bigger than they had ever been and ask, "Do you really mean it?"

"Hugo!" she shouted, seeing that he wasn't paying any attention to her.

She began to walk among the stones that Eusebio had been playing with, then she stopped. No, let him come to me. He has to come to ask my pardon, to explain why he left me here so long. Suddenly and with a horrible clarity and precision she heard something wiggling along the ground near her. She looked down and screamed when she saw a snake. Her whole body was like lead. There was no way to escape, not even the slightest chance of running; and the snake was coming near her, wriggling its body, lifting its head. She could only raise her hands and desperately bury her fingernails in her scalp while she watched the reptile come closer and closer and closer. She cried out again, buried her nails in her skull, and once more cried out.

Hugo, with a stick he had picked up from somewhere that not even he could remember, killed it with a sharp blow on the head. Eusebio came up to look, startled but not knowing exactly why he was startled. He saw the long, greenish-brown body of the snake and noticed that Uncle Hugo was pressing its head with the stick. First a pair of little teeth appeared and then a beautiful green liquid. It was ugly, disagreeable to see, repugnant. And then his uncle picked up the snake's body with the stick and put it close to his aunt's face, laughing; and his aunt began to scream and cry until Uncle Hugo, indignant, threw the snake away among the stones and shouted to her to calm down.

They returned in silence. It was getting dark. Suddenly Uncle Hugo began to swing the car from one side of the road to the other, going faster and faster, and Eusebio was scared and wanted to be close to Papá or Mamá.

"Hugo, you're going to kill us!" Esther shouted.

"So what the hell?" he answered, smiling, and kept on making S's on the narrow road until they reached the house.

"Why did you stay so long?" Lorenza asked.

chapter 19

Esther didn't know whether to be grateful for Aunt Amelia's presence at the table or to be upset because she was there. The roast lamb in her mouth had the consistency of a rag. She kept chewing the same bite without being able to swallow it, then she started to feel nauseated and took several sips of wine. Finally that passed, but now she couldn't use her fork; she was unable to move. And she did not want to be immobile. Aunt Amelia laughed ("Why?" she asked herself. "What could she be laughing at?"), but it didn't relieve the tension in the atmosphere. Lorenza and Gabriel tried to do something about it and began to speak at the same time in strange, quick voices; but Joaquina's face was as tense as before, unchangeable. Esther couldn't see Hugo (he was seated on her left), but she guessed that his face was just like his aunt's, that it had the same expression of hate. "How did it begin today?" she asked herself, concentrating on the window, looking out at the shining cornfields of the communal farm. The calm of Sunday afternoon seemed to exist only out there somewhere, very far away. Esther didn't want to hear them anymore. She wanted to be deaf and not hear any more of the argument.

"Enough for today. We have a guest. Forget it."

As if he were a child, as if he . . . Shall I say something? But what would I say? And suddenly she felt that she was the cause of it all, that she had started it all the night before. When Hugo stopped the car she burst out crying. Gabriel led her to the living room. "Calm down, easy now." But she could not control herself. It was as if she were crying for the first time in her life. She felt Joaquina's hand caressing her; she also was encouraging her to calm down. And instead of helping her it made her weep all the more, made her feel even weaker to be protected by this strong woman who was caressing her tenderly. She felt that she had become the spoiled child that she really never had been and took refuge like a little girl in the attention being given her—attention and love that she would have liked to last indefinitely. Someone brought her a cup of tea, which made her sleepy. She noticed that she was very tired and her eyelids felt heavy. Their words were confused, indistinct. She stayed that way a long time—lying on the sofa—until their words (shouts) woke her up again. Without opening her eyes she understood that she had corroborated Joaquina's point of view, that she had become her accomplice. They had joined forces without saying a word. She had betrayed Hugo.

Throughout the whole morning of the following day Hugo avoided being alone with her. It seemed that he and Joaquina were looking for each other, following each other, dominated by the urgent need to be insulting, to hurt each other, as if the time had come to decide which of the two was boss. Aunt Amelia's arrival was not enough to change the course of events, the argument continued in another form. Disguised, sometimes silent, it grew the way rivers grow when it rains, with a muffled, rumbling force that at any moment may sweep something away—or everything, for that matter.

Hugo stood up, staggered, recovered his equilibrium, and left rapidly. Esther knew that the moment for reconciliation had come, that it depended on her.

"Sit down, Esther," Joaquina ordered. "Leave him alone."

She spent five eternal minutes during which she felt cornered, made into a statue without a will of her own, incapable of moving a single finger. Then Lorenza saved her.

"Let's go downstairs to my living room."

Everyone began to move; she imitated their movements and got up. She caught the meaning of Lorenza's glance, a glance that told her to go look for him. She ran to their bedroom but he wasn't there. She went out to the hall. The door to the entrance was wide open. The sun blinded her and kept her from being sure who was standing in the doorway. Then she made them out: Hugo, Eusebio, Aunt Amelia's chauffeur, and Burgos. She walked slowly, trying to be calm and to smile.

Just as she arrived at the steps she heard Lorenza's piano: Chopin, "Fantaisie in F Major." Esther felt as if a great weight had been lifted from her.

"Where are you going, Uncle Hugo?"

"To play with my pistol. Come on."

She knew that she had to be calm and that she couldn't leave her husband alone. She felt again the distant certainty that was born the first time she heard Joaquina and Hugo arguing in her presence—the certainty, the premonition, the horror of tragedy. Hugo and Eusebio were walking toward the hill, Burgos in front of them. She wondered if she were exaggerating the possible consequences of the argument. Hugo and Joaquina would probably calm down in a hour or two the way they always did. And yet her heart was beating with a nervous rhythm that seemed to foretell something. She was embarrassed because Doña Amelia's chauffeur saw her biting her finger.

"Go on in," she said to him. "Alejandro is in the kitchen. You may eat with him."

The chauffeur assented, expressed his thanks, and went past her. Esther did not move until she heard him enter the kitchen. Her anxiety was growing rapidly. She walked behind her husband on that splendid, unforgettable Sunday afternoon. A wind pregnant with the perfume of all the fruit trees swayed the gossamer pines; the sun's rays cut a diagonal through the little woods. As she walked over the dry leaves, sometimes blinded by the brilliant light that sparkled on the foliage, Eusebio's voice saying, "Shall we hunt for squirrels, Uncle Hugo?" came to her. Burgos barked happily and all the other voices in the kennels echoed him. Esther kept walking until she stopped to rest by the trunk of an oak tree. She watched Hugo breathlessly —he was running, playing with Burgos. The dog was trying to grab the pistol and Hugo, laughing, was making him run from one side to the other. It was the classic game of withholding the bone, testing the dog's agility and patience.

"Okay, that's enough. It's not something to eat," Hugo said and left the gun where Burgos could reach it so he would be convinced that the game was over. Burgos growled. "Be quiet or I'll give you something to growl about."

If I could only get him to give me the pistol, she thought, walking up to him and smiling.

"It's been a long time since we had an afternoon as pretty as this," she exclaimed, holding her hair down, and she kissed Hugo on the cheek before he could evade her. "Okay, let's have target practice. I challenge you."

Hugo staggered. His face was ruddy, his eyes red, the pupils dilated. A ray of sun fell across his face.

"You! Okay." He took her by the hand and, walking rapidly, half dragged her toward Alejandro's house. They entered the darkness of the bar and Hugo picked up an empty cognac bottle.

"Not that one," she protested, frightened. "That's the souvenir."

"Bunk. Let's get going."

The sun blinded her again. She let him lead her, almost running, to the pigsties, where Hugo put the bottle on the fence. Then he took her hand again and they walked away. She heard him counting the steps. "Twelve, thirteen . . . nineteen . . . twenty-five."

Lorenza went ahead of them, trying to hide her own anxiety. She clung to her aunt's arm as if she were afraid that Doña Amelia might go away, and she laughed loudly.

"You know what she says?" she asked with hysterical gaiety. "That she saw so many gringos in New York she thought she was in Mexico City."

Gabriel and Doña Teresa laughed too. Joaquina laughed against her will, and stopped a few steps from the door, but Lorenza went quickly to her with her nicest smile.

"Oh, no," she exclaimed in an affected voice, pretending to be a spoiled child. "Today I'm going to play something special for you Joaquina. My concert this afternoon is in your honor. I can't let you leave us."

They all went in and Lorenza closed the door.

"The light . . . the blinds," she said to her husband, but Gabriel had already opened the curtains and the sun flooded in as if it had been laying siege to the place, waiting for the enemy's first unguarded moment.

The humid atmosphere and the shadows disappeared. All four women saw themselves reflected in the enormous mirror that Lorenza had bought—as a bargain—for twelve thousand pesos. It took up the entire wall and reflected their whole bodies. Lorenza was pleased with her appearance; the design of the silk and the cut of the dress completely hid the fact that she was four months pregnant; and as everybody always said, Lorenza was even prettier when she was pregnant. It was reassuring to know that she was pretty because beauty is the source of a unique security. She again felt that she was mistress of the situation.

Nervous currents, like discharges of electrical energy, ran over her skin and up her spine. The afternoon was like a repetition of a premonitory dream—a tense, urgent situation that she must control because she could rescue it, she could avoid . . . "What?" she asked herself anxiously, as if she were participating in a game where some essential thing had been lost, the key move, the word needed to conjure evil. Her hands moved rapidly over the keyboard, practicing a finger exercise before beginning the piece. Chopin came to her without her thinking about it.

"Serve them some sherry," she asked Gabriel, raising her voice. "I'd like some cognac." She gave him a look full of anxiety, but he seemed not to notice it.

Lorenza heard herself playing faultlessly, her fingers touching the keyboard with professional clarity and precision. She knew that her execution was not perfect because she was using the pedal more than necessary, but her foot reflected her anx-

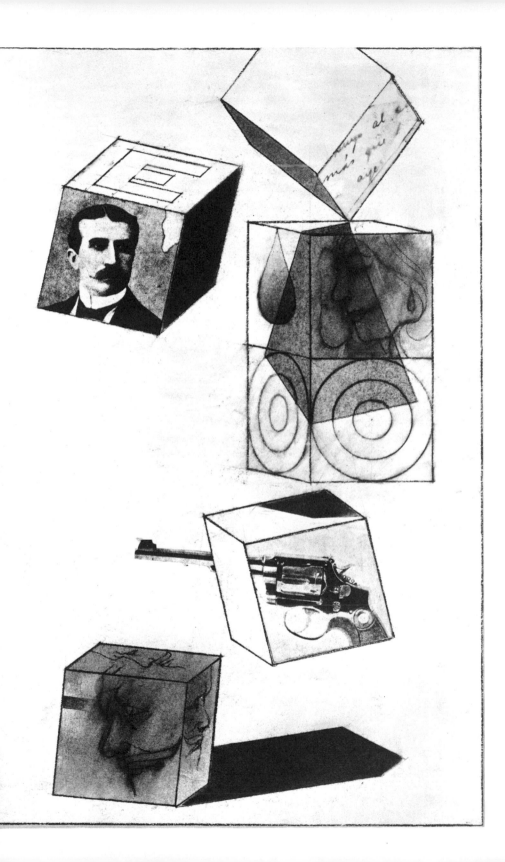

iety, her need for noise. What could Esther be doing? Had she been able to calm him down? Why am I so afraid? This same thing has happened thousands and thousands of times. Could it be my condition? There are women who suffer this way, who are unreasonably hypersensitive. But I have never . . . She smiled at Doña Teresa, who was looking at her fascinated, open mouthed. No, of course not. I tend rather to be peaceful. I don't lose my sense of reality, I don't exaggerate . . . And I haven't drunk enough for my feeling of fear to be the effect of alcohol. If I had drunk too much, Gabriel would have said something to me about it. It was so disagreeable at the table, so tense. Why does Joaquina have to say those things? Why? And they love each other, they adore each other. Apparently everything that happens here, seen objectively later on, is a frightful triviality.

"Go ahead and talk, be gay!" she said with a charming smile. "We came here to help our digestion. You can talk. It's not like a real concert. The performer will not be offended if she hears you laugh. I'd rather you not listen so carefully, so you won't notice my mistakes."

The three women began to talk to each other, but she could not hear what they were saying. They were at some distance from her, sitting on the sofa on the other side of the room, and the stiffness of their postures made her think of a picture, a print from another century. It was a perfect tableau—it seemed *right* to her instantly—in which she and Gabriel could participate. Gabriel was wearing a red corduroy jacket that could be changed in her imagination into a dress coat; his face as she saw him when she looked toward the window had strong classical lines, exactly the model they would use to paint a "country gentleman." The final touch needed to convert the scene into one of those "beautiful" pictures that monthly magazines give to their readers would have been Eusebio. Yes, her son should be there on the carpet playing with his cat or dog. His presence would be the perfect detail. Where could he be? She asked herself the question while looking directly at her husband, but Gabriel was staring at the window as if he had asked himself the same thing. When their eyes met, they consulted each other silently, each asking the other if their son was in any danger. What should they do? What danger? Where is Hugo? Where is Esther?

Lorenza finished the "Fantaisie" and drank her cognac, still looking at her husband. Gabriel came over to her and gave her a cigarette; he leaned over to light it for her and whispered, "Take it easy."

"You have never played so beautifully," exclaimed Doña Teresa, applauding.

"Never so loud, I'm sure," Doña Amelia remarked. She felt she had to keep on talking, should tell a joke or two, should speak immediately, because the stiffness that had followed the argument between Joaquina and Hugo still had not dissipated and if a silence should come over them, it would prove fatal.

"I should like another drink, Gabriel, if you would be so kind. It seems to me an old lady might be allowed to get a little tipsy. You wouldn't be frightened if I drank a bit too much, would you, Joaquina?" And laughing, she began to fabricate. "It's a custom I started at Christmas. I wasn't used to being alone and I thought if I don't belt a few (*Dear God, lying makes me so vulgar. What an expression!*) I'm going to start bawling right here. And so I decided to go out to dinner. I put on a low-cut dress and more make-up than usual as if I were a 'sporting lady.' "

"Amelita, do you mean you . . .?"

"No reason to be surprised. There's no fool like an old fool. Fortunately my age is a better defense than a husband."

"You aren't that old."

"Give Doña Amelia a drink," Joaquina ordered, standing up.

"Wait a minute, Joaquina!" Lorenza asked. "I am going to play your favorite: 'Clair de lune.' Sit down, won't you?"

Many years later Lorenza asked herself (without ever finding the answer) why she had been so certain of danger, why she had insisted so strongly that Joaquina not go out. She began to play Debussy with a serenity diametrically opposed to what she felt at that moment. Between notes she heard a shot. She was startled and so were the others, but strangely she seemed to feel their reaction more intensely than she felt her own. She pretended not to have heard and continued playing slowly, letting her fingers dawdle over the keyboard. She seemed withdrawn, ethereal, and suddenly the four beings who were with her found themselves absorbed in her beauty, in a tranquility that obliged them to listen to her with complete attention, as if she had the key that would explain everything that was happening outside.

The spell lasted several minutes, another shot sounded, and she explained, smiling, "Hugo is having target practice."

She turned her eyes from them and stared at the keys: she saw her Eusebio and sensed danger, knew that something horrible was going to happen—and that she must stay there, calm, calming them, smiling in spite of knowing that her son was in danger. But she was instinctively certain that nothing could be done, that fate had prepared it all, that for many years they had waited to be together in this room, held by fear or by their inability to avoid tragedy, and that it was she who must see that destiny's cycle should run its course, because anyway they (Esther, Hugo, my Eusebio) were very far away, were unreachable, untouchable . . . More shots sounded, more, more, more.

"Wait!" she shouted, keeping Gabriel from moving. "Wait until he finishes."

And she kept on playing, slowly, very slowly, without coming to the end of the piece, repeating a part, then repeating another part, repeating, extending, putting off the moment of finding out what had happened.

She may have heard the footsteps on the staircase before the rest of them. Someone was running, stumbling and bumping against the wall—running blindly without paying proper attention to the steps. Her stiffened fingers struck a tremendous chord at the very moment Esther entered screaming.

"Your car! Lend me the keys!"

Lorenza could see that everything was turning, getting red; Esther's words had been spoken within an enormous bell that repeated and repeated them. I mustn't be absurd, I mustn't be weak, I'm not going to faint, she demanded of herself.

No one saw her fall to the carpet.

"Quick! Quick!" Esther was shouting.

Doña Amelia explained incoherently that her chauffeur had the keys. Gabriel ran toward the kitchen, followed by Esther. Doña Teresa fell to her knees and began to pray, rapidly, confusedly, while Joaquina and Aunt Amelia ran without knowing where they were going.

"No! Toward El Bordo!" Esther directed Gabriel. "I'm sure that's where he went."

"What happened?" Gabriel asked, lighting his cigarette and accelerating rapidly. Before the two of them ran toward the car, before asking any explanation, he had seen Eusebio go into the house with his hands covered with blood. He wanted to run to embrace him, but Esther stopped him. "He's all right, nothing has happened to him. Let's go." Gabriel repeated the question, "What happened?"

"He killed Burgos . . ." Tears filled Esther's eyes. She had held them back too long and now her sobs rushed upward, choking her. She swallowed saliva, threw her head back, and explained: "He wanted us to have target practice. He was very drunk and I played along with the idea because I thought I could calm him down. He wanted to go shoot at the dining room. We went to the hill, I told him I would challenge him, and he put up a bottle. I shot but I didn't even come close and he laughed at me and took the pistol. I don't know what happened to the gun. It stuck. Hugo shot and the bullet didn't come out and this made him even more furious, and when he tried to see what was wrong, a shot came out and I thought he had killed Eusebio." She was crying again, and covered her face.

"Be calm!" begged Gabriel. "Please try to be calm!"

"But he's like a madman! When he saw that the bullet had struck very close to the child he got even worse. He's desperate, Gabriel, he's crazy! He looked at me as if he were going to kill me! And then! If you could have seen his face. I thought he was going to shoot himself or I don't know what! He's suffering, he's suffering terribly! Then he shot at Burgos and I thought it couldn't be true, that I was dreaming it. But at the first shot the dog arched himself and then fell close to us, stretching out and looking at Hugo, and Hugo shot again and again and again. Eusebio and I were shouting, telling him no. And when all the bullets were gone Hugo fell to his knees and bent over the dog and kissed him and caressed him, crying. And suddenly he stood up and began to run toward the garage and I ran after him asking him to wait for me, begging him not to go. But I couldn't catch him, and I wanted to tell him that I am going to have a baby, that I am going to have his child. And he didn't let me tell him! He'll be so happy about it! Hurry, Gabriel, hurry, he has to know! He has to know!"

Gabriel was forcing the accelerator; on the unpaved road the automobile seemed to fly from the top of each little hill. He knew that he couldn't control the car, that it was excessively dangerous to drive so fast, and even more he knew that the day —hazy, imagined always as in a nightmare—had come. At that moment he would have liked to be God, to have the power of rectifying the acts of others; to redeem his brother, to kill himself if necessary in exchange for the life of his little Hugo, of his little brother. He, Gabriel, was also to blame for everything that had happened; he shouldn't have stayed in the living room with the women, waiting for this outcome. He should have run to embrace him, to kiss him, to tell him that they all loved him, that they all adored him. It was what he had always wanted, what they had never given him. He went faster. He saw that the last hill was in front of them (he heard Esther's weeping and it seemed to him that he was hearing the crying of all the other women in the house), and he started slowing down to avoid an accident at the top. At that moment he wanted fervently never to get there, because he knew that Hugo was no longer at El Bordo.

chapter 20

Hans Meyer looked at the roof beams with the eye of a connoisseur, then admired the solidity of the walls, which had surprised him at first. The lines were good, the construction of high quality. Hans stopped thinking of ways to reproach his wife for pulling him out of his peaceful, warm refuge in order to bring him (they arrived after midnight) to such a cold place. He consoled himself with a cognac, and with another, and then asked for one more because he was still shivering, and then a very pretty and serious woman put a bottle by his side and left him in a corner—somewhat darkened—where he could enjoy the drink and contemplate the magnificent construction. How peaceful it was, ideal for a hotel where one could really rest. A hotel for older people, of course, or for convalescents—people who were looking for tranquility, "homey atmosphere" (he thought with a smile as he looked at the flames in the fireplace) —a perfect place for the bored customers who sometimes came to the Nueva Posada de la Suerte. It would be good to have both places; then, when his guests showed the first signs of boredom or when he heard their first complaints, he could say to them: "I have another hotel, a charming place in the mountains, the ideal spot to rest, where the only noise is the crackling of logs in an enormous living room, low roof, tremendous beams . . ." Ah! He savored the rest of his drink and poured another. He was amused to note (the cognac was making him happy) that people were looking at him with curiosity, that his presence

was arousing interest and evoking guarded comments. Finally
a woman came over to him. She was a very thin woman dressed
in black who asked him, adjusting her glasses, "Are you Esther's
father?"

"Her stepfather," he replied curtly, offended. "I am her mother's husband, her second husband."

Taking another sip of brandy, he wondered if the difference
between his age and the age of Esther's mother were not entirely obvious. Then he shrugged his shoulders, answering himself: Clods, hayseeds . . . meddling fools!

"Oh, yes, of course," Luchita Ramírez answered, pretending
to know all about it. "Esther told me. Such a pity, isn't it? So
young and so tragic."

Hans Meyer would have liked to answer quickly with a brilliant phrase that would explain that great tragedies always happen to young people, but it would be throwing pearls before
swine, so he limited his reply to a slight movement of his head.

"Your little girl, that is to say, your daughter . . ." Luchita
Ramírez appeared confused. She was about to say, "Your little
stepgirl," but since it was not a common term, it seemed out of
place, improper. "Esther, I mean the poor widow, is a sea of
tears. She looks like a corpse! Doesn't she?"

Hans Meyer assented.

Luchita Ramírez continued. "The news spread like wildfire.
We—I'm the president of the Guild—we were going to have a
meeting in the parish hall when a little boy came to inform Father Miguel that one of Doña Teresa's sons had been killed at
El Bordo. We were completely dismayed thinking about the
poor mother, and all twenty-four of us—we are twenty-five
counting Doña Teresa—came as soon as we could get here,
wondering and asking each other what could have happened,
which of the two it might be, Gabriel or Hugo? And we remembered that these horrible accidents are nothing new for the poor
mother. You know her husband died that way too. What a terrible experience! What tragedies life can bring! Only God
knows why we are punished this way. But the reasons that move
His divine omnipotence are too great for our small human un-

derstanding. Resignation! That's all we can hope for . . . Look how many people have come. The whole town is here. That's natural, of course, because we all love the Coviellas, they are always so respectable and genteel, always at home where they belong without meddling in the lives of others. The only one who came to town very much was the deceased. He was such a gay young man. Sometimes he drank a little too much but he never forgot his manners—and now they say he had stopped drinking and I'm not surprised. With a good wife like Esther, he became a very proper young man and one of the hardest workers you ever saw. At five-thirty or six in the morning he was already in the corral taking care of the milking and everything. What a blow for the poor family! Doña Joaquina is closed up in her room and won't see anybody. Doña Teresa looks completely gone. And Esther! And Lorenza! And Gabriel! Even the servants are crying their eyes out. And what a cold night this has turned out to be. Of course, we always have cold nights here. You must be freezing since you are used to Cuernavaca. You have a very fine hotel, don't you?"

"One of the best," Hans answered impatiently.

"I'd just love to see Cuernavaca. At the end of the year when we go on the pilgrimage of the Virgin of Guadalupe, I'm going to see if I can get there for just a little while. What's the name of your hotel?"

"La Nueva Posada de la Suerte."

"Oh! What a pretty name!"

Señora Meyer told Doña Teresa that she was going to see if she could do anything for her husband, and she stood up. She could no longer bear the smell of the gardenias, and the blinking of the candles was putting her to sleep. She walked slowly among the groups of people.

("They told me that he wasn't alone in the car."

"Really?"

"Aurorita López saw his wife with him."

"That's very strange.")

("It's her mother . . ."
"Which one?"
"Good evening.")

("They said at first it was Gabriel, because he must argue constantly with that conceited Lorenza."
"I don't know, but I heard there were shots beforehand.")

("He was so young, wasn't he?"
"What do you suppose she'll do now?"
"Well, I don't know, but I understand he tried to kill her."
"No!"
"Yes, there's more here than meets the eye."
"I thought so from the beginning."
"And they say the child is wounded.")

What child? Señora Meyer asked herself as she looked for her husband in the hall. Surely it must be the other brother's child. Hans must be furious for being caught here in this bunch of Indians. It's like a picnic. But it came in very handy for me.

("We need to find Rita. She must know all about it."
"Well, there's no doubt there were shots. Anselmo's children were out walking and they heard them and they also heard a woman's screams."
"They say he was as drunk as a lord."
"It couldn't be. He'd stopped drinking."
"Rita isn't going to tell you anything. She adores them!"
"I'll take care of her. We'll find out all about it."
"They probably pay her good money not to talk."
"Well, of course, with money . . .")

Did he really try to kill her? No, she would have told me. It's obvious she is deeply grieved. The poor child is very pale. What will she do now? I hope she doesn't plan to go back with us. She and Hans hate each other. And what if she does plan to go back with us? I'm her mother, she doesn't have anyone else. What a mess! I wonder if he left her any money? If she has some capital we could do it, but Hans won't want to and I don't want to argue with him. If the sister-in-law hadn't called me we would have had the big scene last night. I'm not going to let that bunch of high livers keep on drinking up the whisky. His so-called friends! I'm dead tired. How I would love to have a bed. Those six hours in the car seemed endless, with him arguing and arguing and defending his friends. Tomorrow we'll see. I'll tell Esther that we have to go after the funeral, because we can't be away from the business. Where could she be?

("They say she's pregnant.")

A child? A grandchild! What would we do with a grandchild! On the other hand, if she does have a child she won't be alone, and it would be better for her to stay here where he brought her. Who'd have expected all these complications? She knows we have very little in common. She doesn't like our friends; she gets bored. The best thing is for us to live apart. Of course she could live with us a few months while she pulls herself together; and then, if he didn't leave her anything, I could set her up in a little business in Mexico City. Hans would agree to that in order to get rid of her . . .

("In little pieces."
"Yes, torn to bits."
"Didn't you see the car?"
"Quiet, here comes Lorenza!")

"Have you seen my husband?" asked Doña Esther.
"He's in the downstairs living room. This way." She pointed to the winding staircase.
"Thank you. I'm going to look for him."
Carefully she descended the stone steps. How in the world did he get here? she asked herself. It's just like him to poke around everywhere. Undoubtedly he has already thought of what a fine hotel this would make. It is a beautiful house, but who would come here? This living room is better than the one upstairs . . . She saw her husband chatting with a skinny woman who looked as if she belonged in a convent, very ugly, un-

questionably a spinster. She admired the lighting fixtures, the enormous mirror, the carpet. And she thought with satisfaction that her fur coat (bought in Berlin) was very appropriate to this elegance. The only advantage of living in a cold climate was being able to wear winter clothing. It's such a pity to keep this coat put away all year long!

The homely woman stood up when she saw her approaching, and her teeth grew large in a smile. She opened her arms and Doña Esther could not avoid her effusions.

"You are the mamá. You know how sorry I am." She kissed her on the cheek. Immediately Luchita Ramírez thought that she had expressed herself incorrectly. How could this lady, this total stranger, know how *she* felt? What she should have said was: "You *don't* know how sorry I am." She made up for her mistake by smiling even more widely and adding, "Your poor little girl! So much in love, just like her husband. And what a cute pair they were. You must be completely worn out."

"I am tired, very tired."

"Of course you are. Ah, these tragedies!"

"And the trip."

"Yes, it's such a distance. But sit down here with your husband."

"What about you?"

"Don't worry about me. I'm like one of the family. I'll go see if I can do something to help the girls. Excuse me, please."

She went away quickly and Doña Esther sat down by Hans.

"This would make a fine hotel."

"I knew you were going to say that."

"Do you think they'll sell it?"

"Hansi! Please remember that I am in no mood to talk about such things now. She is my daughter, my only daughter. Give me a cigarette. I'm overwhelmed by all the things I've heard. What a terrible bunch of people! Do you think there's anything hidden or strange about Hugo's death!"

"I don't think anything, because I'm not in the least interested in it. And you know that perfectly well. Don't bore me."

"Hansi, don't talk so loud."

"Why not? Is there anybody here who knows us?"

"We don't know them but they know us."

"They know your daughter, you mean."

"Well, of course, but my daughter is a member of our family."

"*Your* family."

"Hansi, why are you so sharp with me?"

"No more than you are with my friends."

"Oh!"

Doña Esther inhaled her cigarette and gazed at two little marble statues, two goddesses. Her glance was lost in the folds of their tunics. In the morning she had dreaded the coming of night, because she knew that she and Hans would get into an argument as soon as he found out that she had ordered the bar closed to his friends except when she was present. It was a drastic but absolutely necessary step, because week after week they drank more than a thousand pesos' worth of whisky and cognac. And we simply can't afford it! Hans had no right to protest, but he would protest, and unfortunately she would end up giving in to him. But Hans put up so little money! Really it's all mine. I'm not going to tell him, of course, but that's the truth. After giving the order to the bartender she began to tremble, thinking about the argument that was coming. She tried to be pleasant at dinner time, made over him, was on her best behavior so he would think (before starting to insult her) about what a good wife she was. The fan was running constantly in the terrible heat. As if Hans suspected something, he watched her from time to time out of the corner of his eye, and she felt defeated before the battle started. But she was not going to give in. No. A thousand times, no. Let him spend as much as he wants on himself, that's all right with me. But I'm not going to keep up a bunch of deadbeats, a bunch of pretty-boys who take advantage of his good disposition. Oh, no! That's what really gets me. They show no gratitude whatsoever. They think they deserve it all. Why? At five in the afternoon she thought her heart would burst from fear. She had the presentiment . . . felt the storm coming . . . He was getting more and more disagreeable, as if he already knew. Could the bartender have told him?

And then suddenly, like a salvation from on high, the long distance call came, and the office secretary came to say that it was
for her. Doña Esther ran to the telephone. "From where?" she
asked first. What could she want? she wondered, thinking about
her daughter and remembering that she had not answered her
Christmas card. I've been so busy! Could she be sick? And suddenly a woman's voice and the explanation: "This is Lorenza
Coviella, Esther's sister-in-law . . . Yes . . . No, she is all right . . .
The reason I'm calling is to tell you that Hugo . . . her husband
. . . Hugo . . . was killed in an accident. This afternoon . . . In
the car. He was driving . . . A barranca . . . Yes, she's all right.
He was by himself . . . Esther can't talk now. It was a while
ago . . . I tried to call you." She hung up the telephone and
thought: I have to go, no question about it. She started toward
the pool. A widow! How terrible! I'll have to go there! I'll just
have to go, there's no excuse. It's an obligation. We will have to
be there (she smiled, walked a little faster): *we* will have to . . .
he ought to go with me. He's my husband, and it's his duty. His
cousin can take charge while . . . Yes, it's perfect, that nuisance,
Rody, will be good for something. And Hansi (who had drunk
more than he should have but not more than he was used
to) accepted with the placidity of a drunk who takes everything easily and doesn't care one way or the other. Then it
occurred to her that the argument had been postponed and that
on the way back she would be able to explain convincingly why
she had laid down the law. Yet something told her that she
wasn't going to be able to do it. Something told her that Hans
already knew about her order and was waiting for an oppor-
tune time to bring it up. Well, I will *not* give in to him . . . And
her daughter saved her again.

"I think the poor little thing will have to come to live with
us."

"What?"

"Esther. There's no other way! I'll tell her that we're expecting her, and that as soon as the novena is over she can come to
Cuernavaca . . . to her home. We have to take care of the poor
child. She's so upset! Did you notice her eyes? It frightens me

to think that something could happen to her. May God forbid! We will take care of her"—she used the plural with emphasis— "it's our obligation, Hans. She worked so much and we didn't give her anything. When we settle accounts she must have thirty-three percent."

"Oh, no! You're not going to force her on me again."

"Ssssh! Quiet, dear, quiet! Here she comes. She looks overwhelmed with grief. My poor little girl! I'm going to take care of her."

Excellent! She was leaving him there thinking about Esther. When they argued about other things now, she would bring up her beloved daughter. I've beaten him again! And trying to keep her victory from showing in her face, she kept her eyes on the carpet and walked toward her daughter.

"Can you sleep a little while?" she asked gently.

"Oh, Mamá!"

"Don't be angry, dear. I'm just saying it for your own good."

"Surely *you* want to sleep."

"Not yet. It's still early. I'd like to talk with you a little . . . alone."

"For what?"

"Well, dear . . . that's a strange question. It seems natural enough to me that a mother should want to talk to her daughter."

"I'm not going back with you, if that's what's worrying you."

"Esther, for heaven's sake! How can you be so cruel?"

"Mamá, don't pester me, please."

chapter 21

Joaquina looked at the grass and then raised her eyes slowly, taking in everything: the shrubs, the honeysuckle, the roof tiles, the mirador, the hills, the sky. And she realized that she and her brother Eusebio had had something in common, even though it had never made them feel close to each other: both of them had come to Mexico to *live*; neither of them had ever thought about "the American adventure." And she thought that, of the two of them, her brother was the one who had succeeded. He had lived happily and had died happily (at least in a certain sense, if the circumstances were not taken too literally); he was loved during his lifetime and he was still loved by all who remembered him. And I? Her question fell as a rock falls in a lake and makes larger and larger circles until the water became smooth again. And I? And I? Why didn't I? She thought of the words that Father Miguel had pronounced before Hugo's casket: "Hate creates hate, ill will creates ill will, love creates love, and we will always remember our brother Hugo with love." Yes, I have loved!, her heart shouted. Yes, I do love! Why does love always have to be the same? Why is it impossible to understand that I love? I have loved everything. I've given my life to each thing I've touched. I've loved them all—even Luis, whom I didn't love at first, I even loved him, and very deeply! I haven't been gentle, or kind, my feelings have never been expressed with the facility of this landscape. But you know it, Lola, you knew me well . . . you loved me! And you, too, Luis, you more than anyone! And if I hadn't loved you then and for the rest of my life, I would have married someone else, would have gone to bed with the first man who came along. And now that I'm old it seems foolish to say such things. But they were real, they were very real. I loved you! I still love you! I loved Hugo as if he had been the child we never had! Hate was alive in me before you found me, Luis, that's why I was dry and hard. But I did love. I have always loved. Tell Hugo, please tell him!

She started walking along the garden's abandoned path, saying over and over, "Poor child, she's so young, so alone." The August wind came full of the scent of apples; it spoke of harvest, of fiestas and fairs that bring moments of delight, happy surprises, and pleasant encounters.

Squatting on the bank of the arroyo, Eusebio was sailing paper boats, watching them with sad, new eyes.

Joaquina stopped, leaned against the solid wall of the house, and wept.

Esther went over to the window and opened it wide. She breathed in the peacefulness of the afternoon, the scent of the honeysuckle loaded with blossoms.

"Lorenza," she said, still looking outside, "I'll give you the house. It belongs to you."

Lorenza came over and put her arms around her.

"No," she whispered with a gentle smile that made her look infinitely beautiful. "No, Esther, we want you here. This is your house. It is Hugo's house. My house is in the city. My place is in the city."

"But your son's place is here, your children will belong here."

"Your child will, too."

Esther smiled sadly.

"Well, to get you to accept it, I'll sell it to you."

"Don't talk foolishness," Gabriel said.

chapter 22

She had dreamed that it would begin this way and now, awake in the cold dawn, trembling in the frigid air of her bedroom, she waited to scream again. She waited to hear her own scream, just like the one that had awakened her—long, anguished, herald of the child who was about to be born. She thought, but in a very vague way, that it was still not time, that she still had two months to go . . . And she screamed again. It was another of those screams born of surprise—so much the result of surprise that it seemed not to come from her. She buried her fingers in the pillow. There was a brusque movement, a pain in her abdomen. It astonished her that the sun's rays were coming through the crack in the blind. Everything had an unsettling look of irreality. Like *hearing* her own shouts. Hearing them as if she were someone else. She was glad that her bedroom was separated from the others, because that would keep her from waking up anyone. This is going to take a long time. It's my first one, and they say that the first one . . . She began to sweat.

"Hugo, Hugo, my darling, my beloved husband. The time has come."

Dawn is not coming, she thought, it's already day. How could that be? What time did I wake up? I can't remember anything. Shall I call Joaquina? Can I walk? She moved. Yes, she could. It was very painful, but she could move. Anyway, I have to move, I have to help myself. This could go on for hours. I feel so strange. It seems so different from what I expected. That's natural, of course; they were just ideas . . . Then she screamed again, once, twice, three times. She clutched her face in anguish. It all seemed so unreal, she was screaming without being aware of it; her shouts echoed from wall to wall and still it seemed that no sound came from her lips. She felt pain yet didn't feel it. It seemed that rather than giving birth . . . Another sharp pain and horrible fright. This is it! This must be it!

She kept absolutely still for a few seconds that seemed like hours. Her calm returned and her muscles relaxed; maybe she could keep on sleeping. Her head fell heavily on the pillow, she closed her eyes and thought that she must have been mistaken. It's midnight, dawn hasn't come yet, everything is very dark. I've been imagining things because I don't feel any pain at all.

But then it all happened again. Her shouts echoed and everything was repeated from the beginning. It lasted just a few minutes. It's not me, she thought, but the screams became more frequent—anguished, impetuous, tearing screams. This must be it! I'm not imagining things, my body has a new pain, an unknown warning. And Hugo isn't here! Hugo isn't here to share with me the moment that we dreamed would be for the two of us! She bit her lip, then was aware of a long silence suddenly broken by another scream.

She got up, threw the blankets aside, felt as if she had been freed from an enormous weight. And she was not cold. It's not me. I'm dreaming. There are ghosts here, ghosts invoked by Doña Teresa. She started walking in search of the ghost of Hugo. But this is absurd, she told herself. I can't go around undressed, looking for a ghost with nothing but my nightgown on. She dressed rapidly, still telling herself that it was all a dream, a gigantic joke in which she had to take part without asking questions, so she would get her prize when it was all over. A happy event, a gift! And when it all ended she would be able to close her eyes in blessed sleep without being awakened by more pain. But now she was supposed to walk, to move about, to open the door and run if necessary. Perhaps it all depended on that. Yes! She must run.

She opened the door and met the ghost and the ghost smiled and came toward her putting on an overcoat.

"I'm going to get the doctor," Gabriel said, "it's begun. The same way it was with Eusebio. There isn't time to go to Jalapa."

He went out running. Esther felt her cheek and it was damp with cold sweat. She had thought . . . Silly, so silly, I thought it was *me*, that this was the way it began. It was an enormous relief to her to know that Lorenza was the one who was screaming. She thought of running to see her, but stopped, feeling repugnance and fear. For several seconds she stood in the passageway trembling, telling herself that she must go to her, but laughing at her intention. Lorenza screamed again and she covered her ears with her hands. She couldn't understand that woman who was howling so, she couldn't understand human pain, she couldn't understand Gabriel's absurd anxiety, she couldn't understand anything. Muffled moans joined with consoling words (at that moment quite clear) reached her ears. Murmurs. Words that crawled through her body like ants. A humiliating and disastrous invasion. It was terrible that a being should be born out of the misery of pain. And now here, standing rigidly in the middle of the passageway, she again experienced something that had happened to her a long time ago when she had seen someone with a nervous tic: she started to imitate it, feeling that she was the sick person. So it was that here she felt that she was the one who was giving birth.

She hurried back, opened the entry door—a cold wind struck her face—and began to run desperately, terrified, calling Hugo. She walked on the flowers of her forgotten garden, stumbled, began to weep and continued her flight, climbing the hill clumsily, slipping, falling occasionally, lost, not knowing where the path was. She reached the woods and embraced the trunk of a tree.

There, little by little, she got weaker and weaker, until her legs buckled and she fell on her knees weeping, desperately calling Hugo. She still heard Lorenza's screams and they kept vibrating within her. She tried to remember a prayer, tried to implore God, but Lorenza's pains kept her from it. I don't want to suffer that! She stopped. Yes, I do want to . . . She had no idea of time, thought that she had been there clinging to the tree for hours. The countryside was completely silent. It seemed to her that hours later a car had come. Or did I dream it?

She heard someone open a window in the house, and then another scream escaped through the window. Then, there was still another scream. But, this time there was no doubt about it, it was her own. Esther started running again and got as far as the pigsty, where she stopped, panting, wishing that a prayer would come to her lips, a word that would serve as a key to open the closed world of myth—a world of meanings that were certain, real, comforting.

"The presence of Hugo. My God! Give him to me! Give him back to me!"

She felt an intense pain, thought that she had gone mad, and continued her flight as if suddenly she had been the victim— the chosen one—of an apparition. Illuminated, happy, her eyes transfigured, full of all the light of day, she ran. Her body newly agile.

Gabriel found her in the garden holding a carnation plant that she had just pulled out of the earth.

"Another boy!" he explained, embracing her. "Another boy! He and Lorenza are both fine."

Esther made a grimace that she intended to be a smile.

"Where is the doctor?"

"He's leaving now. But . . . what's wrong, Esther? Are you sick? I'll ask the doctor to wait."

Late in the afternoon Joaquina touched Esther's lips with the glass of brandy that she had asked for. She took a big swallow, but the liquor had no taste. Her weakness stretched a veil over her eyes and blurred the figures of Joaquina and her mother-in-law. At times—when she was able to see them—she was bothered by the slowness of their movements. They were strangers to her, she had nothing in common with them. There was no longer any tie between them. She looked up and saw the roof. I will give the house to Lorenza. She can live, rebuild, invent myths, make a family . . .

Esther looked around her: strange figures, conquerors of all grief, perpetuators of the home, of life.

A month, a week. She didn't know when. Her strength would come back and she would go away, she did not know where.

chapter 23

"Dear Joaquina: We were very glad to get your letter, because we were worried after not hearing from you for two months. Especially me, Joaquina. When I go to bed, while I am giving my son his last drink, I begin to think about you and miss you. Why don't you come back, Joaquina? The house seems empty without you. Sometimes we think we hear your voice, your steps, your words. We need you here. Please don't stay away any longer.

"I would not say this if I weren't sure you would like to be with us, too. You haven't said so, but I know you aren't happy over there. You left because you thought we were reproaching you for something, because you felt that you were to be blamed for what happened. No, dear Joaquina. It is not your fault, or at least no more yours than ours. Gabriel and I talk about Hugo at night. Sometimes we weep. We imagine things, relive what happened, think how easily it all could have been avoided. Lies. We could not have avoided anything. Why do I say so? We all know that Hugo was good—perhaps he was too good, perhaps he was never quite at home with us for precisely that reason. You believe in God, Joaquina; you ought to make peace with yourself. You can laugh at me, at this letter, and think that it is easy to say words. But I'm not just saying words. I have had to suffer what I am writing you. I have wept not only for myself and for the grief of my husband, I have wept for poor Esther, and for you, Joaquina—for you whom I love and understand more than ever.

"Business goes well. Don Saturnino has given me the monthly receipts and the money that you spoke of. Gabriel and I did as you wished and took flowers to Lola on her anniversary; we covered her tomb with carnations.

"We haven't heard any more from Esther. We sent her twenty thousand pesos more than a month ago and asked her to come so we could give her the rest. She is not living with her mother. She rented a furnished apartment in Mexico City. In her last letter she said she didn't know what to do and that she felt very lonely. I told her to come back, and I hope that someday she will, although day by day it seems less probable.

"Doña Teresa had a bad attack of rheumatism. But she is better now, and is here in the living room playing with Eusebio. She asked me to send regards and says she hopes to see you soon. My Eusebio also sends thousands of kisses and wants to know when you are coming back so he'll be sure when to expect the presents that you are bringing him. He wants to know where Spain is and how he can get there.

"My Hugo is precious—he is just like his Uncle Hugo, but he has Don Eusebio's blue eyes and his grandmother is absolutely silly about him.

"Gabriel will write you next week.

"Best regards, all our love, and lots of kisses from all of us. Lorenza."

Joaquina put the letter in her purse for the nth time. She sighed, took a sip of cold coffee, then pushed it away from her. The passersby on the Paseo de las Ramblas moved rapidly before her eyes. Afternoon was falling over Barcelona. Joaquina, her face very pale, like a statue, caressed her purse.